Benita and husband Pip from St Albans have two married daughters and four grandchildren. Benita, former LAMDA teacher/festival adjudicator, is a chimney sweep historian, the author of two books, and Hon treasurer of SWWJ.

Benita writes for stage and screen. Her radio play, *Pick Up,* was broadcast in New York and *Smile Baby Smile*, her short film, was produced in 2013.

To Sharon and Natasha

Benita Cullingford

Edwin and the Climbing Boys

Illustrated by Leona Crawford

AUSTIN MACAULEY PUBLISHERS™

LONDON • CAMBRIDGE • NEW YORK • SHARJAH

A CIP catalogue record for this title is available from the British Library.

ISBN 9781787106758 (Paperback)
ISBN 9781787106765 (E-Book)

www.austinmacauley.com

First Published (2018)
Austin Macauley Publishers Ltd.
25 Canada Square
Canary Wharf
London
E14 5LQ

Acknowledgements

To Alan Durant, Maurice Lyon, The Golden Egg Academy
and Charlise Harding for their help and encouragement.

Prologue

1776, Bay of Biscay. North coast of Spain.

In mid-ocean, a violent storm reached its peak. Lightning struck the *Nancy May,* a merchant ship homeward bound from Turkey. On board, firecracker sparks flew to the night sky. Flaming sails ripped away from the yardarms and spiralled out to sea.

Edwin Richmorton, aged eight, trembled and clutched his mother's skirts as the force of the gale threw them against the ship's rails. The ship floundered. It dipped to starboard, spraying his face with foam from the waves. The *Nancy May* swung back upright again and Edwin heard the shattering *crack* of the mast as it split in two and fell across the bows. The ship carried a cargo of timber and gunpowder. He knew from the shouts of the crew and yells to lower the jollyboat that the ship was doomed.

No time to mourn. Heat scorched his face and smoke clogged his lungs as he screamed for his father, no longer there. His mother grabbed his arm. With minutes to spare, they hugged each other, then held hands and hurled themselves into the waves.

Edwin gasped as the breath left his body. His blood seemed sucked from him by the ocean's coldness and he forced himself to swim. The ship's jollyboat was in the water overcrowded with men from the crew. Edwin reached the boat and held up his arms. He wasn't the only one desperate for help. Next to him, a sailor clung to the side of the boat. He wore a skull and cross bones ring on his index finger.

The sailor swore at him and lashed out with his fist. He felt the ring dig deep into his forehead and blood washed from his face as the sea closed over him…

Strong arms hauled him aboard. In the mountainous waves, he glimpsed his mother. Her outstretched arms, and her dark hair floating around her as she drifted away. He screamed and screamed for her. And he heard the cries of the crew, and probably that of his father, before the *Nancy May* exploded and sank beneath the waves.

Chapter 1
Fire

April 1780, England

"Fire! Fire!"

"Where's the blaze?"

"Bottom of the school field. Cottage chimney fire."

"Out of the way, Richmorton!"

Latin primers fell to the floor. Fellow scholars in vampire gowns shoved Edwin aside as they leapt over benches and dashed from the Abbey School hall.

He sat there unable to move, then his knees trembled as a dreadful fear returned. In his mind's eye, he saw the burning cottage, smelt the smoke and heard flames roaring up the flue. And he imagined them spewing from the chimney pot. Edwin hugged himself and screwed up his eyes, but he couldn't forget the burning sails and horror of the fire at sea. It still haunted him.

After his parents' deaths, he'd been too grief-stricken to care when his uncle, Lord Robert Richmorton and aunt, Lady Elizabeth adopted him. They had no children of their own.

"It will take time. You'll soon forget, dear. Time will heal," said his aunt.

"I say send him to the Abbey School as a boarder," bellowed his uncle, Admiral of the Fleet. "A little Homer and Greek will soon clear his head. What's done is done. Life goes on, don't y' know."

He knew all right. Edwin shuddered and opened his eyes; then he wished he hadn't!

Two bully boys had returned for him. They ran grinning down the hall.

"Richmorton's still here!"

"Hiding like a weak-livered sissy."

Edwin jumped up, his fists clenched ready to defend himself. No fighter, he quivered when they reached him. They were mean-spirited brothers, new to the school with a reputation for terrorising weaker boys. Built like bulldogs and two years older than him.

They grabbed his arms and dragged him outside and across the quadrant to the school field. But Edwin told himself they were cowardly pack-hounds, and he could outrun either of them, given the chance. His brave words got him nowhere when he saw black smoke spiralling up from the cottage chimney. He'd let them take him unresisting, and they'd slackened their hold. With a sudden burst of energy, he surprised them and broke free.

Inside the hall again, Edwin collapsed onto a bench. Sweat dribbled down his face. He dragged a sleeve across his forehead and gradually controlled his breathing. The sun no longer sent coloured patterns across the floor and a chill descended from the rafters. Edwin looked around the ancient abbey hall, with its hanging flags of past chivalry and stained glass windows. And he lowered his gaze to the rows of empty benches and discarded books. Like him abandoned. He'd tried to make friends. But they'd said it often enough: He was an 'oddball, not one of them.'

Things were different when he first joined the school, orphaned and a curiosity, the son of the British Ambassador in Turkey. They'd sat him on the dais; he turned to the platform now, at the top end of the hall. Such disappointment! He'd stared at them stony-eyed, reliving the terror of his night in the ocean; the sea aflame with burning debris and his mother's hair, floating, as she drifted away.

Edwin gave himself a shake and stood up. They'd soon be back from the fire, full of excited chatter, while he remained the same. Well, he was sick of it:

"I'm sick of being myself!" Edwin yelled, glaring at a benevolent-looking friar in a stained glass window.

"Well, my son, do something about it!"

Was he going mad? Did the friar speak to him? "I can't help what's happened, and I can't *make* myself be happy. But I can change, I can try," he said. Was that a nod from the Friar? "I'll be wealthy one day. I don't want to be, but…." His shoulders slumped remembering a conversation he'd overheard.

"He'll do his best, Robert! We must make allowances," said his aunt, sounding unconvinced.

"All very well. He's had long enough. If he doesn't toughen up, things won't bode well for the future." And his elderly uncle had returned to a stint at sea.

Edwin sighed. And then he straightened his shoulders and brightened. No more heart searching. He expanded his chest and grinned at the friar. "I'll make friends and toughen up." Galvanised, Edwin ran down the length of the hall and saluted the chivalry flags, one by one. And then, having decided, he headed out to join in the excitement….

Too late.

They were back. Disappointed scholars surrounded him; their gowns and spirits dampened by rain. A downpour had put out the fire and saved the derelict cottage but it had spoiled their fun.

"Why didn't you come?"

"Afraid to get wet?"

"Afraid the rain would spoil your curls!" He wore his hair to his shoulders.

High above the taunts, a shriller, more mocking voice. "He's a coward. Richmorton is afraid of fire!"

Gideon, the canon's son. That bespectacled little swot! How dare he! A loner like him, he'd confided in him once. Edwin glared at Gideon itching to hit him.

"Fire, fire, fire," they chanted. "The Viscount's afraid of fire!' And they pointed, laughing.

Edwin turned away, his cheeks flaming. It wasn't their jeers. They often made fun of him. They'd ribbed him before about his clumsy bed making. Not his fault, with an Embassy that was full of servants. And he'd balked at eating porridge. Six whacks of the Head boy's cane taught him the folly of that. No, it was his title of Viscount. Mention of the future Dukedom and its responsibilities made him cringe. It was something to live up to. And the worse thing was – his uncle was right. He'd soon be thirteen, almost a man, and he knew nothing of the outside world.

He'd gone over all this, Edwin reminded himself. And he stiffened his shoulders. Several followed him as he left the hall. But he walked tall, and they dwindled away. Fun over.

Edwin flicked his hair back. Gideon had done him a favour; it was the spark he needed. Of course, he wanted to prove himself to his uncle. *Bonitas, scientia et disciplina*: Goodness, knowledge and discipline. He was good at discipline. Right, he'd set himself a challenge. Make a three-fold plan and tackle one task at a time. He'd told the friar he would change; toughen up and make friends. He'd begin with his fear of fire and not let it ruin his life. And he spun round and grinned at the friar.

The back of the cottage faced the school field, and the garden, long neglected, was overgrown with a tangle of nettles and wild rose. Several weeks had passed and this was his first chance to get away unobserved. Edwin stood back from the gate and lifted his gaze to the slate roof. He shaded his eyes against the sun. The chimney pot, blackened one side by the fire, was still intact.

He'd only seen the smoke. The flames had been pure imagination, how pathetic was that! He stamped the ground, mortified. What could he do about it? He stared at the chimney's large buttress on the outside wall and an idea came to him. It was impressive enough to sketch. Architectural drawing was something he was really good at. His mother had encouraged him and even framed a pyramid he'd once drawn at the age of six. It was probably still in the Embassy library.

With the weather still bright, Edwin borrowed a stool from the Abbey kitchen and set off for the school field. He didn't mind who saw him. Most scholars went home at the weekend. Of the few who boarded like he did none followed him, as far as he knew, and he managed a fair sketch of the cottage and chimney buttress.

Later, when alone in his dormitory, he put the drawing under clothes in his portmanteau and pushed it under his bed. As he did so, he wondered if he was trying to hide his fear. Drawing the outside of the chimney wasn't much of a challenge; he should have gone inside the cottage and confronted it. Edwin sat on the edge of his bed and pondered.

Not for long. He grinned and jerked his legs in the air. He could study the chimney flue and note its construction. Perhaps even climb the chimney! Exciting. Dangerous. Whitsuntide holidays in two weeks, he could do it then.

A sudden noise made him look up. The smile left his face. Oh, no! The bully boys. They were thumping up the stairs. Edwin dived to the floor and squeezed under the bed with the fluff and his portmanteau.

The bully boys charged into the dormitory shouting:

"You can't hide from us!"

"We'll get you, rich boy." Edwin pinched his nose to stop himself sneezing.

"Yeah, next term we'll lock you up in that old cottage."

"Leave you there to starve."

"Hee, hee, hee." They found that hilarious and screeched like marauding hyenas.

Then there was silence.

They'd gone. Edwin waited a few minutes then he crawled out from under the bed and stood upright. He wasn't trembling, he told himself. They still hadn't got him. So, they'd seen him go to the cottage and do his drawing. Well he didn't care; he might have a few qualms but he'd decided to climb the cottage chimney. Edwin stared ahead unblinking. It would be the first task of his challenge and nothing would stop him.

Chapter 2
First Climb

Edwin stood inside the large kitchen fireplace. School term was over. He'd left his portmanteau at the Abbey gateway and raced down to the cottage. This was the start of his plan to change. He'd thought about it long enough. Time to get going.

Bits of charred rubble lay at his feet; relics of the fire – believed lit by vagrants. Edwin raised his chin and stared at the blackness above the hearth. His stomach tightened. He could do this. He'd climbed trees in the abbey orchard. They were old and stubby but good practice and better than nothing.

He removed his frockcoat, didn't fold it, and dropped it to the dusty floor. His first act of rebellion. Within reach, high on the left side of the hearth there was a protruding iron ring. Edwin fingered the medallion he wore round his neck; a keepsake of his parents never worn at school, then he gripped the ring with both hands and hauled himself up. Using elbows and knees he scrambled over the stepped shoulder of the chimney breast and entered the flue.

It was dark, far darker than he'd imagined. He couldn't see anything! His arms shot out and hit the sides of the flue. They were smooth with hardened tar. His nose wrinkled at the sickly smell. Bile rose from his stomach. He swallowed hard. It wasn't the smell; it was fear, threatening to overpower him. He squeezed his legs together, wanting to pee. Where's the sky! Why couldn't he see the sky? Desperate for light, he straddled the flue with his arms and legs and climbed crab-like. The flue sloped backward and curved away. He shouted aloud, just to hear his own voice: 'The bend, the bend! I must reach the bend!'

His stockings wrinkled down. His foot slipped, and a sharp pain pierced his knee. The flue narrowed and his bunched elbows and knees knocked the sides scraping his skin. Cold sweat ran down his face. 'I can't stop now,' he wailed. He tried another tactic and bridged the gap with his body. With bent knees and feet flat against the side of the flue he pushed back and inched his way up. Somehow, he squeezed round the bend. Just a short stretch of flue. Then a puff of air, and above him – a circle of sky. He cried out in relief, 'I can make it,' he yelled.

A muffled peel of bells reached his ears. Evensong! He should be on his way home by now. Old Amos would be waiting at the Abbey gateway with the chaise, his aunt's mare snorting and hoofing the cobbles.

Climbing upwards again, his fingers found the rim of the chimney pot. He scrunched his shoulders, squeezed through – and just made it as the pot, damaged by the fire, crumbled apart. He collapsed to the roof tiles, and the evening air hit his lungs sending him into a spasm of coughing. When he'd recovered, Edwin sat on the roof ridge hugging himself. He couldn't stop grinning. It was unbelievable that he'd achieved something at last. He pummelled his knees in glee. He'd climbed the chimney; his first step in conquering his fear of fire. Everyone should know. Mary should know. His cousin Mary was the only one who'd care. He wanted to throw his arms in the air and yell across the miles, all the way to London,

"Mary, look at me now!"

The Abbey blocked his view. It dominated the top of the hill, his ancient school fortress-like beside it. Edwin's chin dropped to his chest, and he stared at the rips in his breeches and blood on his knees. Had he really achieved anything? Painful and unpleasant, yes, but the chimney hadn't been that difficult to climb. He wasn't *physically* weak. Fast on his feet and a good swimmer, he'd even taught Mary, three years older, to swim. Edwin reminded himself that he'd climbed the chimney flue when he *knew* it had been on fire, and he straightened his shoulders. From his position, he spotted the abbey gateway. No sign of Amos. Edwin chuckled, guessing the old groom would be in the nearest tavern. He swung his legs over the roof ridge and turned around.

A breeze buffeted his face. There was a *swoosh* of wings and a jackdaw settled further along the ridge. He flapped his hand at the bird. The jackdaw lifted a foot and stepped sideways towards him. "I'm king here!" Edwin shouted. The jackdaw gave him a beaky glare, waltzed closer, then extended its wings and soared away.

No competition.

Edwin shaded his eyes and squinted into the distance. He could see the wheat-fields and dark wood curtaining his uncle's estate, and he groaned. The lonely mansion was the last place on earth he wanted to spend his school holiday. With his uncle still at sea, and his aunt busy with her new house in London, apart from the servants he'd be the only one there.

Edwin pulled his stockings up. He couldn't do anything about his torn clothes or his knee; they'd have to wait. After a long term at school his breeches had worn thin, anyway. He braced himself for the climb down. It might be difficult, he thought, lowering his legs into the pot. But in the empty mood he was in, he didn't care what happened to him.

When he dropped to the hearth, steely fingers clamped his shoulders.

"Got you, you varmint!"

His feet left the ground as someone violently shook him. The voice was menacing "No-one climbs them chimneys, but us! We got the contract!"

He winced with pain. Before he could cry out, another voice intervened. The fingers relaxed, and he fell with a *thump* to the floor. He lay there, the room spinning, too stunned to move.

There was a brief silence, then an argument broke out. Through his blurred vision, he saw two boys, one tall and thin and older than the other. The smaller boy had a deep voice. He watched them yelling at each other. Were they arguing about him? Their strong London accents made their speech impossible to follow, and they were mismatched in every way.

While the older boy, who'd grabbed him, pranced about shrieking insults, the smaller boy stood legs apart in tattered knee-length breeches. He clutched a short-handled scraper and soot sack, and looked, Edwin thought, well able to defend himself. He was right. It was obvious who'd won when the older boy's crippled left foot gave way and he stumbled back.

Edwin eased himself to a sitting position. He ached all over. Despite the boy's assault, he felt sorry for him. Judging by the inward turn of his ankle and high arched boot, he guessed the boy had a clubbed foot. He'd seen one before, at the Embassy, when a boy aged about fifteen was regularly carried up and down the main staircase and he'd asked what was wrong with him. How molly-coddled!

The older boy, noticing him move, came and stood over him. "You ain't going nowhere," he said, raising his fist.

"No, I..." Edwin found his voice. "Where have you come from? I mean, how d..."

The younger boy answered for him. "We was jus' passin', and we saw yer on the roof. Didn't we, Jake?"

Jake seemed to lose interest. He slouched to the far wall and slid down; skinny legs outstretched, like a disjointed scarecrow.

The younger boy approached him. "What's yer name?" he said.

The boy looked friendly enough in his black rags, and they could be about the same age. Edwin staggered to his feet. He was taller than the boy. He straightened his waistcoat and replied, "Edwin Richmorton from Richmorton H-all." His voice cracked.

The boys shrieked with delight. The younger one dropped his scraper and slapped his thigh. Jake jerked his legs in the air and pointed a finger at him. Their merriment lasted sometime.

Jake, wiping tears from his face with his coat tails, asked, "What's your Honour doing 'ere then?"

"Oh, nothing much, just thought I'd have a climb of the chimney, that's all." He gave a half-shrug. He felt confident because he was standing while Jake sprawled on the floor.

"You dun right, choosing a short chimbley, ain't no difficulties there," the younger boy informed him. The boy stared beyond him. He'd noticed his frock coat. He grinned, then he let out a whoop and snatched it from the floor.

"See here, Jake. See what we got here. This here's a young gent. A right posh 'un. This'll suit me regular, that it will."

The boy paraded around the kitchen in the coat. The coat tails almost touched the floor, but he wore it with such pride, it made little difference.

"Mistress'll soon have it off you."

"Who says?"

"I says. Bad Bess will leather you proper."

"Not if she don't know, she won't. Not when it's in me sack. She won't know nothink about it. This 'ere young gent won't tell her, will you, mister?"

"Eddie, call me Eddie," he said, the name popped in his head – a new identity. "I promise not to tell anyone. And you may keep the coat."

The boy removed his woollen cap, and his soot-blackened hair stood up in tufts. "I take that as a right kindly gesture." He shrugged off the coat and stuffed it in his sack.

Jake pulled a large handkerchief from his waistcoat pocket and blew into it making a disgusting sound. "One brat begging from another brat," he said, with a scornful look on his face. He looked at Edwin, then got to his feet and stood tall over him. "You treat me respeckful." A bony finger prodded him in the chest. "Now, what you got for me?"

Edwin thought wildly. He bent down and pulled off his buckled shoes. "Here, you can have these."

Jake took a shoe from him. He spat on it and wiped it clean with the edge of his coat tails. The smaller boy tugged at his arm, eager, looking up at him.

"You'd get a lot of rhino for that, Jake. That's good leather there." He whistled.

Jake shook him off and moved to the window. It held no glass, just two planks nailed across. Jake spat on the shoe again and polished the metal buckle to a high sheen. Edwin watched him cradle the shoe. He seemed entranced, turning it in his hand. A slant of evening light shone on the silver buckle making it twinkle. Like the eye of a small trapped bird, thought Edwin. It was an odd thought to have and he wondered if it had something to do with Jake's expression.

Jake turned and flung the shoe at him. "I ain't no softie," he said, and he wrenched the door open, and limped outside.

"I'd best get after 'im." The younger sweep seemed anxious to leave and collected his tools. "Quit moonin'," he said, giving Edwin a nudge. "It don't do no good." He tucked the scraper in his belt and humped the soot sack over his shoulder.

Edwin's chest tightened. He jerked forward. "Where are you going?"

"You don't wanna know."

"I might." He did, he really did.

"London town." The boy grinned. And he ran out, slamming the door behind him.

Edwin stared round the empty kitchen.

They'd gone.

The boys had gone! But they couldn't go, not so soon. He paced the kitchen thumping his thighs with his fists. They were free spirits, companions, with places to go, things to do – achievement. This was his chance to make friends, and it was slipping away. He jammed on his shoes and ran from the kitchen.

He halted outside. To his left, a rough brick path, with foot high weeds between the cracks. It led to an alleyway at the side the cottage. The boys must have gone that way. In front of him, his route home lay across the school field and the Abbey Gateway where Amos was waiting.

Chapter 3
A New Acquaintance

Edwin turned his back on the school field and ignoring his painful knees ran stiffly down the alleyway out into the street. He had no idea what would befall him if he caught up with the boys and went to London, or even if they'd have him! But it would help his plan. He'd experience life beyond the Abbey. Anything was better than spending another holiday alone, in his uncle's mansion.

The younger climbing boy was waiting.

Something clutched Edwin's heart, and he walked towards him. "Mind if I come with you?" Edwin asked.

"You didn't ought to run with those scrapes," the boy said, pointing at Edwin's knees. He bent down and eyed them critically. "You'll 'ave t' rub some brine in."

Edwin blushed, ashamed of his soft white skin. Embarrassed by the boy's concern he changed the subject. "What's your name then?"

The boy straightened up grinning. "Smudge," he said. "On account of me face."

The evening was not yet dark enough for lamps to be lit, but Edwin still couldn't see what he meant. A shapeless cap covered the boy's head and soot disguised all other features.

Edwin held out his hand. "Pleased to make your acquaintance, Smudge."

"Likewise. Ed, wasn't it?"

"Yes, Eddie Hall." The new name was growing on him.

The sound of approaching hooves and the smell of hot horseflesh filled the air. Smudge left him and darted across the narrow cobbled street. He leapt onto the high pavement, just as the coach and four horses careered past. Edwin watched, astonished, as Smudge stood on one hand and stuck out his tongue. The boisterous party of well-dressed gentlefolk laughed and waved from the windows. The coach driver shouted, "Blackamoor monkey!" Several loose stones bounced past Edwin as the coach swayed out of sight down the street.

On the opposite side where the pavement was several feet higher, three steps had been inserted to assist coach passengers. Edwin crossed over and joined Smudge on the top step.

As they walked up the steep winding street, Edwin congratulated Smudge saying, "That was a neat trick."

Smudge sniffed and adjusted his sack. "No rhino, though."

"What's rhino?"

"Blimey! Where you bin?"

"Do you mean money?"

"'Course, what else?"

They reached the last bend in the street, where the road divided. To the right it curved round the Abbey, passing the Gateway. In front of them, the street, crowded with coaching inns and taverns, continued upwards to the Clock Tower and market thoroughfare of St Albans.

As they headed towards the clock tower, with Smudge leading, Edwin suddenly remembered Amos. The Woolpack Inn – Amos's favourite drinking house! If they continued on their present route, they would reach— As though reading his mind; Smudge grabbed his arm and pushed him into a side alley.

"Don't let him catch a sniff of us," he said.

There was an excited urgency in Smudge's voice. He motioned to Edwin to stay well back and cautiously poked his head around the corner. He waited several seconds then beckoned.

"Who's there?" Edwin whispered.

Smudge, grinning devilishly, told him to see for himself. Edwin, unused to cowering in alleyways, stepped out and looked up the street.

The lanky figure of Jake lounged against the Market Cross.

Edwin re-joined Smudge, who hopped about with excitement. "Don't you want him to see you?" Edwin asked.

"Let's trick him. He's waiting fer me to come up the street. If we was to cut round the Abbey, we'd be into Holywell Hill sooner than he could turn round."

"Where are we going, exactly?"

"Gaddwell Priory. We always spends the night there. Come on, look lively!"

They kept an eye on Jake and darted across the street. Out of sight, they ran towards the Abbey. Edwin forgot about his knees and outpaced Smudge as they raced down the outside of the Abbey's long nave. They left the Abbey precincts and paused for breath in Holywell Hill.

Opposite them was The Bull Inn and through the archway posts, lay the entrance to Gaddwell Lane.

The hill was steep and hard work for packhorses with cumbersome loads. The boys waited some time before crossing. As they passed between the wooden posts at the side of the inn, Edwin glanced upwards. The painted bull on the Inn sign stared down at him. In the bull's eye was a half-moon of white. Edwin turned away and almost collided with an elderly man emerging backwards through a side door.

"And next time bring your manners with you," shrieked a woman from inside the Inn. She gave a final shove and out tumbled Amos, who fell, and lay spread-eagled on the ground.

Smudge helped him up. "You all right, Mister?"

"Don't need no help from the likes of you," grumbled Amos, flapping at Smudge with his riding crop. "You leave me be. I can get on me pins in me own way."

Edwin had hidden behind a horse trough. He saw Smudge looking round for him and beckoned him over. The boys chuckled at the sight of Amos straightening his clothes. His wig was lop-sided and his whip had entangled itself in the back of his breeches. To Edwin's relief the elderly groom eventually tottered back through the archway into Holywell Hill.

The boys quickly left the yard. The stench from horse manure, rotting vegetables and fouled straw, combined with that of outdoor privy, was overwhelming. Edwin couldn't wait to get away.

As they walked at a more leisurely pace down Gaddwell Lane, Smudge asked Edwin about Amos; he wanted to know about the old groom and why he'd hidden from him. Edwin didn't answer straight away; he wasn't sure what to tell him.

Smudge persisted. "You might as well spit it out. You running away?"

It was no good. He'd have to know. "I suppose I am running away," he said. "Or I will be, if I stay with you. That's if you'll have me," he added.

They had reached the Goat Inn at the side of the track. Smudge dumped his sack and took a good look at him. Edwin knew his stockings were round his ankles, nothing new about that; his legs were so thin he was forever pulling them up. His shoes were scuffed, and his waistcoat minus a button. Both knees were bloodied and his hands, and probably his face streaked with soot. As Smudge circled around him, he remembered the tear in the back of his breeches.

"So, you reckon you're fit to be a chummy then?" Smudge said, as though the very idea was ridiculous.

"I… I'm not sure. What's a chummy?"

Smudge picked up his sack. As they continued down the lane, he explained. "A chummy is what you is. At least it's what the likes of me and Jake, and the others, is. We was born to it. It's like this, see." As Smudge warmed to the subject, the words tumbled out. "First you got to have a master. You ain't no chummy less'n you got a master. Though master ain't much, not ours ain't – mistress now, she took over from him. Bad Bess be a tough 'un. Tougher than a whole lot of masters."

Edwin wasn't sure what to make of this. He liked the idea of being a chummy, though. It sounded like some kind of friendship gang. Just what he needed.

Evening dew began to fall, and it got chilly. The large sack on Smudge's back was bouncing about as he talked, and Edwin couldn't stop thinking about his coat. Smudge didn't appear to be cold, though, and his legs and feet were bare.

"We has to climb chimbleys and scrape 'em down," Smudge was saying. "Jake now, he don't climb no more on account of he's a journeyman, an' it were always worse fer 'im, wiv his foot. Jake be out of his time now, and he thinks we got to toady to him." Smudge chuckled. "That's a laugh, that is."

A rabbit shot across their path. It reached the safety of a small copse, then stopped and turned. It stood upright on its hind legs waffling its nose in their direction.

"Jake's proper daft about them creatures," Smudge remarked. "He'd sooner pet 'em than eat them."

Edwin felt the same. An abundance of rabbit, guinea fowl and pheasant was eaten on the estate and he hated having to accompany his uncle on shooting parties to kill them.

The track they were following led to a fast-running stream and wooden bridge. As they stopped on the bridge, Edwin wanted to know more about Jake, and he asked if Jake had completed his apprenticeship.

Smudge removed his cap and scratched his head. "Well now," he said slowly, as though puzzling it out. 'Suppose that might be the case, suppose he might have. Might well be." He seemed bemused by the idea.

"What about you? Are you an apprentice?"

"Never was. I ain't never been 'prenticed. On account of I ain't been with more than one master fer long. I had three masters afore this one. And I been with Bad Bess now near two years."

"Will you stay?"

"Depends."

"On what?"

"Whether I gets the urge to move on."

Edwin picked up a stone and hurled it into the water. Nothing seemed to bother Smudge and he could do as he pleased. "Have you never been to school?" he asked as they left the bridge.

"What for?"

Edwin didn't reply. They walked in silence until they reached Gaddwell Farm at the side of the Priory.

"That's our doss house for the night." Smudge pointed to a tall barn on their left. "I'm going for vittels. You stay here." He thrust his sack at Edwin and headed down a path.

Edwin watched him go then he hoisted the sack on his shoulder and followed. The sack was unexpectedly heavy. It must hold more than his coat! He conjured up a few possibilities; silver plate, a snuff box perhaps, or jewels! His Aunt Elizabeth twinkled with priceless jewels; he'd never seen her unadorned. Climbing boys like Smudge would have easy access to homes of the wealthy. What an intriguing thought!

The path led between sheep pens and a low wooden fence. It was getting dark but he could tell that there were rows of leaf vegetables beyond the fence by their shape, and the smell of cabbage. He could see the Priory on the far side of a stretch of lawn and walked towards it.

Smudge was standing in front of a small purpose-built aperture in the Priory stonework. Above his head was a row of narrow arched windows and to his right a recessed doorway. As Edwin approached, a lantern light flickered in the aperture and a face appeared; a crinkled face framed by a white bonnet. Edwin froze. His hands flew to his face. Sister Ignatius. His aunt knew her. She might even recognise him! He crept across the lawn and hid in the shadow of the doorway.

Smudge's gravelly voice cut through the night air. "I thank your Holiness Missus for these vittels, and Heaven and all. An' I promise to return the platter."

Edwin couldn't help grinning. He allowed a few minutes to pass then he sneaked up on Smudge. The boy leapt forward and almost dropped the platter of food.

"Lummy, Ed! I thought you was a blooming gentleman outer."

"A what?"

"A footpad, Booby."

Edwin laughed. "You don't get me there! I know all there is to know about Jack Hall."

"Who's he?"

"Have you never heard of Jack Hall?" Smudge shook his head.

"He was a chimney sweep like you, then he turned highwayman and was hanged at Tyburn."

"When was that?"

"December, 1707." Edwin did a quick calculation, "Seventy-three years ago."

"One of your family, was he?"

"No. I'm borrowing his name, though." He gave Smudge a grin, "For as long as it suits."

Smudge seemed satisfied and Edwin decided he liked the young sweep. He asked few questions and seemed content with simple answers.

When they entered the barn, the interior smelt dry and musty, and to Edwin's unaccustomed eyes appeared empty. Smudge, however, knew better. He nodded to some dried up wheat sheaves stacked in a corner. Still holding the platter, he swept an arm across his chest in a mock bow, and announced, "Upper berth or lower, your Highness?"

A tall shadow stepped forward and snatched the platter. "What you got there, you mangy nipper?" It was Jake.

Edwin swung the sack he still carried, and he and Smudge wrestled Jake to the ground. As they rolled about in the wheat sheaves, the tough straw spiked his face and one of his ears got crushed. The rough combat was something he'd never experienced. He felt charged with new excitement. No one won. It wasn't that sort of fight – just a jumble of arms and legs; squeals, cusses, and straw. Edwin got to his feet, pink in the face, thrilled.

It was all over. Jake took charge. A draught of ale in The Goat Inn had put him in a good mood. He retrieved the scattered food, broke the rye bread in half, did the same to the cheese, and then handed a portion of each to Smudge. He kept the rest for himself.

"You brought him along," Jake said, jerking his head at Edwin. "So you'll have to share." He added a warning, "Don't forget we've got a foggy hole tomorrow."

Edwin protested but Smudge generously crumbled his portions on the surface of the platter and divided the pile into two. They ate in silence. High in the rafters, a barn owl pretended to sleep. When Jake had finished eating, he dragged a bale of straw some distance away and settled down. Smudge joined him.

Left on his own Edwin re-arranged the straw. He used his folded waistcoat as a pillow and fell into a fitful sleep. As he dreamed, images of his aunt and Jake hovered above him. His aunt's handsome features interchanged with those of Jake. Jake's long fingers jabbed at him. His aunt's soft voice whispered first in one ear then the other. A flutter swished past his face. Jake's lanky hair trailed away…

Edwin jerked awake. Once again, the inquisitive owl circled the barn then returned to the rafters. Edwin settled back with a sigh. This time he slept well.

When he woke in the morning, both Jake and Smudge had gone.

Chapter 4
London Connections

Mary leapt from the chaise too fast for Amos's help and shouted for the groom. As the lad approached, she instructed him to see to the horse and direct Amos to her aunt's kitchen. She then gathered up her skirts and ran towards the mansion. Her long legs soon covered the distance.

Lady Elizabeth Richmorton's new London residence was finished at last. No scaffolding remained, stonemasons, bricklayers and carpenters all departed. Years in the planning, the imposing mansion designed and built to her aunt's specifications occupied one corner of Portman Square. At the front of the house, a large area laid to lawn. Outwardly, all was ready.

Within minutes, Mary was through the servants' quarters, up the back stairs and into the front parlour, her light blonde hair streaming behind her.

Her aunt stood in the centre of a sunlit room. Surrounded by exquisite furnishings and delicate figurines she looked elegant and composed. Mary could hear her mother's words ringing in her head.

'My dear sister-in-law will entertain there, bestowed with the best that money can buy. In time, all London Society will dine at her table.'

The sun's rays picked out auburn tints in her hair, and her beauty made Mary despair of her own appearance. She bobbed a greeting to her aunt and hastily re-arranged her skirts.

Elizabeth glided forward. "Mary, dearest child, my favourite niece," she cried, planting a feathery kiss on both her cheeks.

"Why, how hot you are! And so early in the day. Whatever ails you? I, myself, might come over all of a flutter, if I so much as dared to think of the upper apartments and the decoration still be done." She lifted a hand to her brow.

"Aunt Elizabeth…"

"Now come to the window and let the breeze cool you."

"Please listen…"

"Dearest, calm yourself. I can't have agitation in my beautiful new room – it upsets the ambience so."

Mary squeezed her hands together to control herself, and appealed again. "In that case, Aunt, *please* may we talk in the garden?"

"Good gracious, child, by all means." Elizabeth's flawless brow creased in alarm. "Is it poor dear Charlotte?" She pushed open the glass doors and stepped out onto the balcony. "How very fortunate she is to have such a daughter." Her for-get-me-not blue eyes misted over.

"No, Aunt," Mary said, firmly, "I assure you Mama is well enough. But I've come here in haste with Amos…"

"Amos?" Elizabeth interrupted her.

"He's waiting to take me back." Her voice rose in urgency. "I've come to tell you about Edwin."

"Edwin?" Her aunt couldn't have looked more surprised. "Why, what can possibly be wrong with Edwin?"

"He's missing. He must have gone off somewhere and no-one seems to know where he is!"

Elizabeth gasped. Her natural colour drained away and two blobs of red stood out on either cheek. "Continue, if you please," she whispered.

"It appears, that when Amos took the chaise to the school yesterday, he found Edwin's portmanteau by the Abbey gateway but Edwin nowhere to be seen. Later, when Amos went back to Richmorton Hall, the servants reported that Edwin wasn't there. He'd still not returned this morning," she added.

Elizabeth sank down on the balustrade. "Then surely, he must have stayed the night with a friend." A stray ringlet uncoiled from the pile on her head.

Mary frowned. As far as she knew, Edwin had no friends.

"That's where he'll be," Elizabeth cried, capturing the curl and tucking it back. "Edwin will have gone to the house of that boy... What was his name? Giddy something or other, the canon's son." She patted Mary's arm. "He'll be there."

"But, Aunt," Mary persisted, "Shouldn't Edwin be here with you, now that you've moved to London?"

"Let me recollect," Elizabeth said, looking vague. "Of course, plans have advanced considerably. Edwin may not be fully aware... Dear me, how inconsiderate I am! Tell me, dear, when did Edwin's school term end?"

Mary turned away, shaking her head. Her aunt knew so little about Edwin. It was kind of her aunt and uncle to adopt him after his parents' death. They had no children of their own and it must be difficult for them. She remembered how much she'd enjoyed Edwin's visits from Turkey, and how sad that the friendly child had changed since then into a lonely secretive boy... Even so...

Elizabeth interrupted her thoughts. "It was good of you to come and let me know, dear. I'm sure you are worrying unduly, and we'll hear from him soon."

Her aunt brightened. A small figure stood in the doorway; a black child dressed as a flunky. He wore blue satin shirt and breeches, and the whiteness of his stockings matched his grin. On his woolly head was a powdered periwig.

Elizabeth smiled and beckoned. The little boy approached carrying a bowl of fruit. He offered his mistress an orange. Then turning to Mary, he said with a saucy look, "Pretty Missy want orange?"

Mary scowled. Her aunt laughed and pulled the boy to her. She whispered in his ear making his brown eyes roll.

Mary swung away. If her aunt hadn't been there, she would have stuck her tongue out. She hated the way her aunt favoured him. As it was, before saying something she'd regret, she blurted out, "Perhaps if you'll excuse me, Aunt, I should be going."

"You're leaving, my dear? Why, you have barely arrived! And I've so much to show you..."

Her voice trailed away.

Back in the chaise, heading north to Islington, Mary remembered Edwin's portmanteau. She questioned Amos further. At first, the old groom seemed reluctant to say anything. Finally, he told her that:

"Being worried and with no instructions what to do," he'd had some discussion about it with cook. "And they'd got a gardener to prise it open."

"Very sensible. Edwin may have left a message," Mary assured him.

"No Miss Mary, we only found his clothes and a drawing of a cottage chimney. Cook thought it were the old cottage where chimney caught fire."

"Where is this cottage?"

"Edge of school field, Miss Mary."

That would make sense, Mary thought. Scholars weren't allowed out of school grounds during term time. By the time they reached her parents' country house in Islington she'd formed a plan.

While Amos waited outside the drive gates she quietly collected her pony, Rats, from the stable. The idea was to tether Rats behind the chaise and continue with Amos to St Albans. Then she'd visit the cottage. If it was the last thing Edwin had sketched there may be a clue to his whereabouts. She wasn't bothered about the time she'd be away. Her mother, confined to her bedroom, wouldn't be expecting her back from London until late. And she'd achieve much more if she brought news of Edwin.

With Rats finally tethered, they set out north again. Rats, furious, had set up such a clattering of hooves it took Mary a while to console him. She'd explained that a return journey with her on his back would be too tiring. An apple persuaded him.

On arrival at the Abbey gates, Mary left firm instructions. She told Amos to hurry to Richmorton Hall. If Edwin was there, then a servant should depart post-haste to Islington with a message for her parents. Amos himself had done enough that day. The elderly groom agreed.

Anxious thoughts flashed through her mind as she galloped Rats across the school field. What if Edwin was still in the cottage? Had fallen. Become ill. Kidnapped! Townsfolk used the field during school holidays.

Mary left Rats to graze and made her way through the neglected garden at the back of the cottage. She glanced up at the roof. Broken chimney pot and blackened one side. It must the one Amos mentioned, and the cottage was the only cottage bordering the field. A boarded up window, door unlocked and off its hinges: obviously derelict. No harm looking inside, she decided.

Her heartbeat quickened. She daren't think about what she was doing. It was enough being out unaccompanied without her parents' knowledge, let alone following a whim and entering –

Her shoulders slumped in disappointment. A dim, dusty room. Nobody there.

She'd been buoyed with anticipation and the cottage was empty. What she'd expected to find she didn't know; more than a hearth full of rubble and burnt ashes. All this way for nothing. Mary scowled and kicked the rubble with her riding boot. How could she have been so foolish?

Then she spotted something.

A glint of silver. She stooped and picked it up. It was Edwin's medallion and chain. The one he wore round his neck. Mary clutched the medallion to her chest. She recognised the engraved profile of Edwin's mother and father. Her mother, Charlotte, had given Edwin the medallion when all his parents' belongings were lost at sea, and the little boy had nothing tangible to remember them by. Mary wiped away a tear. She knew how much it was treasured.

"At least I've found it. And I'll keep it safe," she told Rats, stroking his velvet nose. She leaned her cheek against his flank. The chain wasn't broken, just unclasped. But what was it doing there? She wondered. And where was Edwin? A frightening thought. Perhaps he *had* been kidnapped. The wealthy heir of an Admiral would fetch a high ransom.

Rats gave a neigh. Mary swung herself up in the sidesaddle. Enough time lost. She had to hurry back to Islington. She urged her pony into a fast gallop.

By the time they reached Hagbush Lane Rats had had enough. Mary slowed him to trot. She leaned forward and patted his damp neck.

"Forgive me, Rats," she murmured, "I shouldn't take my worries out on you."

Rats snorted and flicked his ears; whether in agreement or not, she couldn't be sure. She and her pony were often at odds. Rats lowered his neck and whinnied. Taken unawares by the sudden movement, she fell forward against the pommel.

"Steady boy!" She patted his neck, and then sat back, righting herself. A gunshot sound from the hedgerow, and a rabbit shot across their path. Rats reared and stumbled forward, tripping on hard ruts in the lane. The extra movement threw Mary sideways off the pony. She cried out, half prone on the ground, her foot still trapped in the stirrup.

As though from nowhere, two children appeared.

"Help the lady, Pete." A slim, softly spoken boy held Rats by the reins, quietening him.

Mary kept still, while Pete's little fingers unbuttoned her boot and eased her foot free.

"I've made your stocking all dirty," the child said, kneeling beside her. "Joe and me," he said, "We try and keep clean but we've no soap. We used to—"

"Pete, don't bother the lady. If she's not hurt we'll be on our way."

Mary looked from one to the other. They were alike. Both had sandy hair cut to a ragged bob and were poorly dressed. Brothers, she decided. Pete had outrageous ears. She guessed he was about six years old and his face didn't seem strong enough to support them.

Pete sat beside her on the path and whispered, "Can I rest here with you? Joe will let me."

Mary looked at the older boy, who shrugged, resigned, but remained apart. She called out, asking if they had been on the road long.

"Since four this morning, and we've still some distance to go." Joe's voice had no discernible accent. "Its best he doesn't sleep now. We promised mistress we wouldn't be late."

"Late for what?"

"We've two more chimneys to core."

Pete's eyes were closing, "I've been up and down, Joe," he mumbled. "One was werry clean, no..." His head slumped forward.

Mary reached for her boot. "If you're going to Islington, he could ride with me. Rats won't mind."

Mary tried to make conversation, but it was difficult perched sidesaddle, with little Pete asleep in front of her, his head between the pony's ears. Joe walked ahead, slim and upright in threadbare clothes. Joe's thin shoes slapped the dust. There'd been no rain for weeks and the sun was sinking. Her mother would be anxious by now. More to herself than Joe she unburdened her thoughts.

"Mother's such a responsibility. She's never well. We have a nurse, but mother likes me to look after her... She usually gets up when the *Quarterly Review* arrives. She likes to read of the war, and the shipping news. She helps father that way. Mother has plenty of time lying in bed, and father has the bank to attend to."

Joe turned around, "What bank is that?"

"Wilde's Bank."

"Close by the Fleet?"

"Yes, I'm Mary Wilde. Do you know of it?"

"We wash there, in the river."

Mary's cheeks burned; she wished she'd said nothing.

The first of several houses came into view. Rats stopped and his ears twitched.

"Your pony wants to canter," Joe said matter-of-factly. "And we're near enough now."

Pete sat up looking perky. "That was fun," he said, stroking Rat's ears. "What's he called?"

"Rats."

Pete grinned. "That's a funny name."

"I call him that because he likes kicking the stable rats when they annoy him." Mary said.

"Can we have a donkey, Joe, *please*?"

Joe smiled, "If you save your pennies." Pete slid to the ground. "Thank the lady, Pete."

"When we get a donkey, you can ride it," he promised her. And he ran to catch up with Joe. Then they were gone.

Mary moved Rats slowly along. Her ankle still ached. The children intrigued her, especially Joe, and she wished she knew more about them. She understood what they meant by 'coring.' Her aunt Elizabeth had talked of having the new chimneys in Richmorton House, cored. She explained they had to be cleared of masonry and rubble before fires were lit.

As Rats trotted passed the grand houses of the new Packington estate, Mary found herself looking up at the chimneystacks. She'd never noticed them before. Joe and Pete, or just Pete? She wondered. Which chimneys would they be climbing?

Poor little Pete, while he'd been sleeping she'd had time to study his ears. Compared to her pony's velvet coverings the little boy's calloused ears looked thin and vulnerable, though the coating of soot may have offered some protection.

The boys had taken her mind off Edwin. She sat up straight and gave the reins a jerk. As they dashed passed Islington Green her fears for him returned. She was fond of her cousin. "I must find out what's has happened to him," she muttered. Perhaps her father would help.

Chapter 5
What to Do?

Edwin had left the Priory barn. But not got far.

When he woke that morning and discovered he was on his own he couldn't believe the boys weren't there. He'd scattered the wheat sheaves, desperately searching for some sign of them. Even crumbs from their supper would've been something! Nothing but mouse droppings; no Smudge, no Jake, no sack, no empty platter from the Priory kitchen. No proof that the climbing boys had ever been there. He even wondered if the events the night before had ever happened. Had he been dreaming? Was he kidnapped? Even as he thought it, Edwin knew he was being fanciful. In his wildest imaginings, when he'd longed for a friend, he could never have invented a boy like Smudge.

Daylight filtered under the barn doors. Edwin re-stacked the wheat sheaves in recompense, in case anyone found him. How would he explain his presence? He needed a wash and his coat was missing. Should he say someone had robbed him? He bent down and peered through a knothole in the door. The barn faced sideways to the path and the bridge and stream were within running distance. He could escape!

Edwin pushed the doors apart and – ran straight into three nuns, patiently waiting. They marched him to the priory garden, a determined sister holding each arm. A much younger nun followed behind. She had news.

"He warned us," she said. The older boy, the one in charge." Her voice rose in excitement. "He said a gentry's runaway was hiding in the barn." Edwin stiffened. The nuns halted, waiting for him to say something. He pressed his lips tight. The young nun continued.

"He wanted no responsibility for him." That's what he said.

Edwin sat on the garden bench offering no resistance. He bent forward, his hands clasped between his knees wondering what to say. He'd not uttered a word since his capture. The nuns fluttered their hands and raised their eyebrows at each other. "Who is he?" He heard them whisper. "What shall we do?"

"I'll fetch Sister Ignatius," one of them said, and she hurried away. The younger nun, who wore the clothes of a novice, sat down beside him. She kept peering at him and he sensed she didn't know what to make of him. The blood rushed to his face. He turned away from her and stared around. Where could he go? Sister Ignatius was coming. She might recognise him! He furtively studied the garden. Rows of neat carrot tops ahead; cabbages to the right, to the left, onions, and next to the onions – soot, he smelt it – a pile of fresh soot!

He was off…

"Oh, NO!" squealed the young nun.

Edwin darted towards the soot heap. He heedlessly trampled a path of onion tops and dived into the pile head first. When he emerged, choking and coughing, his nostrils flaring with soot, three nuns were staring at him aghast. He shook himself and sneezed. Powdery soot flew everywhere. The nuns screamed and backed away. To them no doubt he resembled a fiend from hell.

Edwin sprang from the heap. He snatched up a two-pronged fork and charged towards them. The young nun fell to her knees in prayer. The others turned and fled.

Edwin threw down the fork. He felt sorry for the young nun who was trembling. He bent over her. "Sister," he whispered, "You have nothing to fear from me." She looked at him, startled. He held her gaze, half-smiling trying to reassure her.

"Where are you from?" she asked, getting to her feet.

"I'd rather not say, at present. But I need your help, Sister." He picked up the fork. "I'll help you with the gardening."

"Why should you do that?"

"In payment for food and information. I need to find the boys who spoke to you this morning. What time did they leave?"

"Before seven. But…" she hesitated, "They have no need of you."

"Did they say that?"

"The older one did."

"Jake?" prompted Edwin. She nodded. "Well, I'm not surprised. They stick together, those two. The younger boy stole my coat."

There was a movement beyond the fence. Edwin raised the fork.

"I'm quite safe, Sisters," shouted the young nun. "He means me no harm."

There was a whispered exchange and Sister Ignatious pointed in his direction. Edwin picked up a handful of soot and tossed it around. "Where do you want this?"

"No, don't use that!" cried the nun. "It's still fresh and much too acrid. If you want to help, use the old soot over in the pen." She hitched up her skirts and showed him what to do.

What a fool! It must be obvious he was no chimney sweep.

It was some time later, and Edwin felt hot and fidgety. He'd spread all the soot and re-planted the onions. While working with the young nun they'd remained silent, and he knew nothing further about the boys. Judging from the height of the sun, by now they must have had several hours start, and he'd no idea in which direction! It was time to go.

"Sister, are you going to help me?" he asked, bending down close to her.

The nun straightened up and wiped her brow with her apron. "Well, you could do with a good wash. I can see that. I'll fetch water."

"I'll wash in the stream," Edwin said. Anxious to find out, he asked her about the boys.

"They sweep the Priory chimneys," she said, turning away.

He stood in front of her and tried again. "Sister, how do they travel?"

"With the farmers. The farmers take grain and other produce into London and return with soot. We need little soot, but the wheat farmers use several tons of it," she explained seeing his puzzled look. "Did you not know?"

No, of course he didn't know. And he turned away and glared down at the dirt path at his feet, hoping she wouldn't question him. A small circle of glass caught his attention. It was the top of a wine bottle. His relations drank wine at every meal. Edwin moistened his lips with his tongue wondering if he'd ever taste wine again. For a miserable moment, he even considered going home, and his shoulders slumped. Bottled up with excited tension, events had happened and he'd responded without thought. Now, like uncorked wine, his energy was draining away.

The young nun seemed surprised by his dejection and became friendly. "They brought us some sea-fish, once, from London," she said.

Edwin perked up. "Billingsgate?" he asked. She shrugged and shook her head. "Well, thank you, Sister. That's something to go on." He beamed at her, then lifted his hand in a farewell gesture and moved away.

On reaching the low fence marking the Priory boundary Edwin vaulted over and set off across the meadow.

"Wait!" He stopped and glanced back. "I've remembered," shouted the nun. "I believe they're Mr Carter's boys."

Edwin whooped and spun round with his arms in the air. "Bless you, Sister. Bless you!" he shrieked.

At the far side of the meadow the grass sloped down to a small bridge over a stream, containing beds of watercress. Edwin rushed over the bridge and fell full length into the water. He'd gulped down several mouthfuls before remembering his shoes. He kicked them off and threw them to the grass bank. With no rain for weeks at a time, the clear running waters were low. They scarcely reached his waist. Deep enough though. He lay on his back; his itchy body floating above the pebbles. Heavenly!

Overhead, a pair of off shore seagulls dipped lower to take a peep. They circled, uncertain, and then were gone. Trails of dark water oozed from Edwin's clothes and a wriggle of tadpoles fled in disgust. Watching them Edwin recalled his mother's dark hair floating… He sat up with a jolt. Sad memories, he supposed, would never fade. But then, should they?

Edwin stretched out on the grass. The sun still shone and he felt wonderfully clean, even if he didn't look it! His dive into the soot pile had been quite an experience. Altogether, he reflected, not unpleasant. Discounting the sulphurous smell and the itchiness afterwards, the heap itself was feathery soft and fine – like baker's flour, only black.

His white stockings were filthy. He pulled them off, squeezed out as much water as possible then lay them flat to dry.

A sudden chill overcame him.

His fingers clutched his neck, felt all round, then down his shirt front. His medallion and chain? They'd gone! Where was his medallion? He bent forward and raked his hair. He scrambled to his feet, stripping off clothes; his waistcoat and shirt, his sodden breeches, searching, searching. He couldn't have lost his medallion… He let out a cry of anguish, "Got-to-be-somewhere."

Edwin threw himself down on the bank, buried his face in the grass and thumped the ground with his fists. Uppermost in his mind was the thought Smudge had stolen it.

Edwin pulled himself together. He knelt upright and stared into the distance. It was hard not to cry, but he was no longer weak, he told himself.

Fully dressed again he felt calmer. And calmness helped him think. What if it wasn't Smudge? His mind raced with possibilities: the tussle with the boys in the barn, his dive into the soot heap, or more likely – his medallion could have washed away in the stream.

The stream flowed into the River Lea. If he followed the course of the river south he'd reach Islington village, on the outskirts of London. His cousin Mary lived in Islington. But then, how could he explain? She'd never understand. Edwin sighed. He admired his cousin. Mary was fearless, she would never have to prove herself.

"I've a lot of growing up to do before I meet my cousin," he informed a startled grasshopper, who leapt away. "Voicing thoughts is good for the spirit," he shouted.

Energised again, Edwin set off, not exactly joyful, but inspired by a new goal. Smudge may or may not have taken his medallion, but he had to find out.

Chapter 6
Friend and Foe

At Cole Harbour Wharf, a barge had caught fire. The landlord of the Three Swans Tavern close to the towpath had passed a jug of ale to the bargee when a shout came from the roof above.

"Barge on fire!" Smudge, high on the tavern chimney, could see down into the hold of one of the barges where fire licked the coal dust.

The tavern emptied of clients; Jake first through the door with empty sacks. Smudge slid down from the tavern roof. As he sprang onto the barge, Jake waded into the canal. He passed the waterlogged sacks to Smudge and climbed aboard himself. The boys then descended into the hold.

The crowd on the quayside waited. A cloud of dirty smoke ballooned skywards. The boys emerged and everyone cheered.

The bargee stammered his thanks, and Jake and Smudge were honourably escorted back to the tavern.

The waft of smoke reached Edwin's nostrils from across the meadow. He'd been heading for Cole Harbour Wharf hoping to catch a riverboat to London, but he smelt fire and instinctively turned back. Why? He asked himself, as he hurried along the highway. Why was he still afraid of fire? His footsteps slowed and he paused to think about it. During winter months at Richmorton Hall, he'd kept away from the huge logs with their leaping flames. He preferred the unheated library. But things were different now; he'd conquered his childish fear when he climbed the cottage chimney. Edwin squared his shoulders. He'd be brave and head for the wharf again.

No sooner had he turned back, when out of nowhere, the highway became crowded and dusty with country folk going in the same direction. Presumably heading for London. A groaning wagon piled with logs forced him into the hedgerow. Then he had to wait while a string of mules plodded passed. Their panniers bulged with goods and he ran ahead to keep from the stench of hot flanks and flicking tails.

He'd walked several miles when he reached a crossroads. The sun beat down on his head and there was no shade. There was, however, a triangle of grass where he could lean his back against a milestone. The milestone read: TEN MILES TO LONDON. Edwin sat on the grass and groaned. Ten miles! He wiped his forehead with his sleeve. His shoes rubbed, and he was tired already!

The pleasant sound of *clip clopping* made him spin round. An ancient horse came trotting along the path towards him. It was harnessed to a small cart carrying sacks of straw and bundles of wood faggots.

"Good day to you, young fellow," an elderly farmer called out.

The horse ambled to a stop. Then, from behind the cart, three large white geese appeared. They traversed the cart and the horse, then waddled across the highway and continued down the lane opposite, one behind the other, seemingly, it appeared to Edwin, going about their own business.

"They knows the way," chuckled the farmer, his red-veined cheeks wobbling beneath ginger eyebrows. "We're off up to London City. You heading our way?"

Edwin leapt to his feet. What luck! "I'd be most grateful for a ride, sir," he replied, and he shook the surprised farmer by the hand.

Fitted to the cart was a rough wood bench. It made uncomfortable seating, but he was too happy to care. The old horse put on an extra spurt and soon caught up with the geese. From then on, both horse and farmer seemed content to amble along, taking their time from the geese.

"How do they know which way to go?" Edwin asked.

"They two daft ones, they follows Blackfoot. He's the leader," said the farmer, adding with a certain pride, "I've had that Blackfoot three years or more. He do a good job." He chuckled. "He's the master all right."

"Really?"

"Gets quite upset, if he don't get his walk, each week; cackles for minutes on end. And he don't mind walking in winter. We puts shoes on him, else his feet get sore."

Edwin tried to imagine this, and he was just about to ask, when the farmer added proudly, "My wife makes him little boots out of canvas."

After travelling companionably for some miles, they reached the suburbs of London. Edwin noticed that a number of terraces had been built, and the town houses became taller the closer they got to Islington. Remembering that Mary and his relatives lived in Islington, Edwin quickly slipped from the bench to the floor of the cart where there was less chance he'd be spotted. He needn't have worried. At that moment, without any guidance from his master, the old horse turned down a cobbled street on their left-hand side and halted outside a chandler's shop.

It was their first stop, and Edwin helped the farmer unload the cart and carry bundles of wood faggots into the shop. The chandler's was well stocked, not only with candles, but ropes and canvass for seafarers, as well as equipment for other trades. Edwin took a good look around. Trading in his buckle shoes for a steel scraper and pair of canvas slip-ons seemed a good idea.

He did this while the farmer walked the horse and cart to the end of the street where they could turn round. Edwin tucked the scraper into his waistband, as he remembered seeing Smudge do. The chandler gave him three silver pennies in change, which he placed in the toe of one of his stockings.

With the faggot bundles gone, he could hide in the cart, if necessary. There were even some empty sacks. Back on the main highway, the geese had carried on walking. The old horse had to trot at a fast pace before catching up with them.

"I seen that scraper what you bought," said the farmer. "And you've a thatch of black curls," he joked, "Just the thing for a chimney flue!"

The farmer may be unschooled, but he was observant, thought Edwin. It must be obvious to him now, that he was a runaway. "I've a mind to learn the trade," he muttered. He glanced down at the roadside, assessing the distance, wondering if he need jump from the cart. He must have looked nervous because the farmer turned to face him and make amends.

"Now don't you worry, lad," he said. "You'll have your own reasons. And I'm not one for prying."

After continuing on for some time, the farmer's head began to droop. Edwin didn't blame him. The horse's pace was so slow he found it difficult to keep awake himself.

They were passing the conical tower of the New River Head when the old horse spotted a water trough. He trotted over, took a couple of spluttering gulps then stopped with his head poised to one side as though listening.

The geese were waiting. Blackfoot sniffed the air then he lowered his neck and made a legs-splayed, dash for the water trough. When he reached it, he reared on tiptoe and opened his wings. The other geese honked approval and did the same. With all three geese flapping and squawking, it was quite a display. The old horse backed away, and the geese took over the trough. They drank together, creating a synchronised ballet of head bobbing.

Edwin couldn't enjoy the show. He remained low in the cart, hidden under the sacks, wary of the Quaker workhouse at the side of the road. They might be on the lookout for stray boys!

As they neared Smithfield, the road filled up with livestock of all descriptions. The geese bunched up, trying to keep together. At one stage, when a flock of sheep threatened to separate them, Blackfoot caused such a flapping commotion that the entire flock parted down the centre like a woolly tide. Eventually, though, the geese had to be rescued. The farmer pulled into Charterhouse yard, then, with surprising agility for his age, he ran ahead of Blackfoot and waved his arms. Several foot travellers joined in the fun. The geese were quickly captured and confined to the cart.

Edwin judged it a good time to leave. He thanked the friendly farmer who good-naturedly gave him one of his sacks, and they parted company.

In the bustling thoroughfare of Cheapside, horse-carriages clattered backwards and forwards. Edwin had to push his way through hawkers of wares on the sidewalk. His ears rang with the noisy cries around him, and he had no idea where he was going.

At the entrance to Milk Street he came across a blind countrywoman selling curds and whey. She sat behind a tub brimming with curdled milk. In front of her waiting their turn, were a group of urchins. Edwin clamped a hand to his mouth and his heart almost leapt from his chest. There were chimney sweeps among them! His head pounded with hope as he stared at each in turn. Too much to ask! None of them resembled Smudge, but they might know of him.

When it was his turn, the old woman kept her head bent, her jaw working from side to side as she fumbled for Edwin's change. As he turned away with his bowl, one of the sweeps spoke up:

"Now there's a sootie what done well!"

"I warrant you he's not from round these parts. Ain't that so, bruvver?" said another.

As they edged towards him, he noticed that the sack on his shoulder contrasted strangely with theirs and his mouth went dry. He clutched his bowl and gulped down the watery curds.

"Good, eh?" one of the boys enquired.

Edwin wiped his mouth on his sack. "Not bad, I s'pose," he said, coarsening his voice.

It seemed to work. The young sweeps pressed around him.

"I'm looking for Smudge," he said. Several soot-black faces began to titter. "Or Jake, mebbe… Foreman Jake." Now they laughed openly, and started to chant:

"Jake, Jake, Foreman Jake, what a rake! State your stake…"

"Mr Carter's boys," he shouted.

The voices fell silent. Edwin sensed a movement behind him. His heart nearly stopped as a heavy hand clamped his shoulder.

"Oo's arsking?" said a hoarse, unpleasant voice.

Edwin held his breath, trying not to tremble. One by one, the young sweeps slipped away. The blind woman craned her neck round in their direction. She opened her toothless gums and spat:

"'S 'at you. Scurvy Sam?"

"Shut your face!" said the voice.

"Eh! eh! eh! 'Tis Scurvy Sam." The old woman cackled with delight, her sightless eyes lost in puffs of skin.

"I arst – oo's arsking?" said the voice again.

The hand pressed hard on Edwin's shoulder, and his knees buckled. He slid his eyes sideways. A large leathery hand, smelling of the sea. A sailor's hand with calloused knuckles and a ring on the index finger. Edwin's nostrils flared. He'd seen that ring before. The terror he first felt turned to rage. He swung round. A giant of a man towered above him. Edwin glared at the buckle on his wide leather belt.

"I'm known as Edwin Hall. And I'm looking for Mr Carter," he said through gritted teeth.

A criss-cross map of a face with sprouting stubble, replaced the belt. The eyes were cold and fathomless.

"You a sweep, boy?"

Edwin jerked away. The giant reeked of rum. Edwin couldn't recall what happened after that. A blow to the back of his head sent him unconscious to the pavement.

When he became aware of his surroundings again, a rope round his waist was pulling him along. The dingy street they were in smelt like a sewer. He staggered behind Scurvy Sam, remembering his name despite the throbbing pain in his head.

Something else was niggling him; something he desperately wanted to remember, but his mind was too fuzzy.

Sam led the way between two derelict warehouses. They backed onto Fleet Ditch. Here the stench was worse. Edwin swallowed a mouthful of bile that rose from his stomach. No time to be sick as he followed Sam across a makeshift bridge. The bridge, little more than two rickety planks placed across the water, sagged and bounced with their weight. Edwin glanced down. The blackish brown water was edged with foaming sludge.

On the opposite bank, a rotting old house overhung the ditch. Sam gave the rope a final tug bringing him up close while he untied the knot.

"Bide your time in there. I'll be back to'morra," Sam growled, giving him a shove.

Edwin staggered backwards into a dim room. The door slammed, and he heard the key turn in the lock. The keyhole emptied. He felt sick from the blow to his head and he couldn't focus. Shouting out and pummelling the door with his fists would make his headache worse. Edwin rubbed his eyes and forced himself to concentrate. Squinting through the keyhole he could just make out the big sailor in the foggy darkness. His knees trembled. Sam had removed the bridge. He'd pulled the long heavy planks back across the ditch and dumped them in a bed of nettles.

"You'll not lift those on your own," he shouted, kicking Edwin's door as he passed.

He wasn't alone! A family of rats sat twitching in a corner. When he turned towards them, they crowded on top of each other squealing in panic. He gave them a glare. There was something endearing, however, about the little family, seemingly trapped as he was. If he showed no aggression, they might leave him alone. He slid to the floor and hugged his knees. His eyelids drooped, befuddled and weary he wanted to sleep. Not yet. He jerked upright, he had to get out of there.

There were no windows in the small room. An oblong cut-a-way in the ceiling offered the only means of escape. Rubbish littered the floor. There were piles of splintered wood and rusty nails, coils of thin steel and a scattering of soiled rags; all too small to be any use. Edwin rummaged around, looking for a strong box or some kind of ladder to stand on. It was hopeless. He couldn't reach the ceiling. There was no way out.

The rats were foraging as well. He barricaded himself from them with some of the larger pieces of wood and settled down. Sleep would be difficult. The blow to his head made him feel lop-sided and fuzzy. He tried to clear his mind.

So much had happened since he'd climbed the cottage chimney... He dozed fitfully, waking every few minutes, then dozing again. Smudge and Jake; friends or foes? The young nun... the farmer and the geese, no, goose. A black-footed goose. He tried a chuckle but the back of his head felt as though trapped in mortar.

The rats scurried around. Edwin fidgeted. What would happen to him when Sam returned? Would Sam sell him to a Master sweep? Sam was a sailor, and more likely take him to sea or force him to work on a lighter boat, unloading coal. Something was biting his thigh! He sat up. It was too dark to see. No beady eyes anywhere, even so he couldn't help shivering and his thoughts returned to Sam. The ring on his finger, why remember that? Had he seen it before? Eventually, overcome with tiredness he fell asleep.

Chapter 7
Mudlarks

The following morning, Edwin half opened his eyes to the sound of church bells; some close, some distant. Several seconds passed before he realised he wasn't at school, preparing for Sunday morning attendance in the Abbey.

The rat family bared their teeth. Unknown to Edwin he was lying on their hole. They wanted to attack him but he reeked of soot. Warm meat, however....

A sharp pain brought Edwin fully awake. He sprang to his feet. Two baby rats clung to his curls. He prized them free and dashed them to the floor. The rest scattered squealing in all directions. Edwin broke out in a sweat. Had the rats bitten him? He'd die of the plague! ... Then he remembered his scraper. No wonder he'd slept badly, the sharp point had buried itself in his thigh. He gingerly removed it. Phew! No bites after all!

It went quiet. Had the rats disappeared? Edwin glanced around. One of the weaker babies lay twitching at his feet. He brought the scraper down, sharp, severing its head. He couldn't bear to see it suffering. Where were the others? He shovelled a pile of rubbish to one side, and in doing so uncovered a neat hole in a floorboard. The floorboard plank was short. He scraped away at the grime and found more short planks, then an edging and – most important of all – an iron ring.

His stomach tensed in excitement as he grasped the ring with both hands and heaved. Nothing happened. What a fool! His weight was holding the trapdoor down. If he stood beyond the door, he might get enough leverage... Should he widen the rat hole instead? A possibility, but it would take forever.

Edwin searched for the hinges. They were deep set and encrusted with dirt. After scraping them clean, he worked his way round the edge of the door. He then gripped the ring again, and with one tremendous effort yanked upwards straightening his legs as he did so… A creak, a rush of foul air and a crack appeared. He jammed in a piece of wood to hold it open and collapsed on his back.

He sprang to his feet. Now he could lift the trapdoor. It crashed back sending nails and debris spinning across the floor. A rickety ladder led to a space below. As Edwin climbed down, his scraper clinked with the coins in his stocking.

The dank room he found himself in showed signs of recent flooding. Green slime covered lower sections of the walls and he had to tread carefully to avoid slipping. In one corner was a square of rusty grating. Set low in the wall, water was seeping through the grating's holes. A way out, perhaps? It must lead somewhere. Some kind of sewer! But what else could he do? He hadn't much choice. Should he remain where he was, and risk being kidnapped by Sam and forced to work somewhere, or chance the sewers?

Edwin prised the grating from the wall and squeezed through. Before he could stop himself, he fell, slithering downwards on his backside in a swoosh of effluent and tidal water. The tunnel narrowed, throwing him sideways, plunging him half drowned past other outlets. He fought to hold his head high, gasping for air, powerless against the downward surge of sewerage. He screwed his eyes tight, not wanting to see what bobbed around him.

Water sucked away from his body, and he found himself up on his knees, his head a few inches from the tunnel roof. A moment of calm. Another gush of water and he fell prone again, face down, being carried along. His mouth was open, gasping. Something caught in his throat. He couldn't gulp it down. The tunnel widened, and he crawled from the foul water, gagging, to the side of the sewer. He stuck a finger in his mouth and retched, sicking up whatever-it-was from his gullet. On either side of him, the walls glistened with slime. He faced the flowing effluent again and forced himself forward.

Then leapt back. What seemed like thousands of bobbing heads with glittering eyes and whiskers came rushing towards him. An avalanche of squealing rats. He turned and crouched low, hands spread, protecting his head. Keep still, keep still. They were escaping the rising tide and as terrified as he was. He held his breath and prayed. Then he squealed himself as the rats scrambled over him, and their claws dug in his back. Swept off his feet by a surge of water, his world blackened.

"A dead 'un 'in it?" said a thin querulous voice.

"Looks like it, Ma." Edwin felt a prod near his spine. "Not long gone, neither," said the child, giving him a dig in the ribs.

He lay on the mud-bank. Now and then, a frill of scum lapped around him. Mud coated his entire body. His eyes refused to open and he couldn't lift his arms, but his ribs felt sore. He'd got feelings so he must be alive. And he could hear voices.

Others had joined the old woman and child. Edwin's arm rose up from the mud. Someone threw water in his face and he opened his eyes. They rushed towards him. The old woman got shoved aside and several hands lifted him free of the mud. Voices babbled around him:

"Said it weren't no dog! Looks like a boy... I seen him first... No you never... Lord love us! Give me a proper fright he did... where d'ee come from..."

Edwin's befuddled mind slowly cleared. He'd no idea what had happened, but no pain anywhere, no broken limbs. Unless mud held him together! Someone handed him a soggy rag.

"Give yer face a wipe," said a childish voice at his waist. It was a tiny girl wearing a muddy sack. "It was me what give you a poke. If I'd knowed you was alive I'd never 'ave done it."

"Let me at him," screeched the old lady, elbowing her way forward. She took possession of Edwin, picking debris from his hair and clothes and examining them. Her teeth chattered in excitement at the bulge in his stocking. Edwin slapped her twiggy fingers.

"Get away!" he yelled, startling himself and the wretched folk around him.

Recognising the authority in his voice they slumped back to their tasks. Edwin stared at them, horrified. They were mainly old women and young children, wearing tattered rags stiffened to boards with dirt. Some carried baskets, others old tin kettles. He watched as they groped about with their hands or prodded the mud with sharpened sticks, isolated from each other. There was no shout of joy on discovering a piece of rag or lump of coal, rather a weary glance about, guarding a find. A more pitiful way of living he couldn't imagine.

Edwin shaded his eyes and looked out to the further reaches of the Thames. Early morning mist hung low over the water, but it had lifted enough, and he could just make out the hull of a tall-masted schooner. He thought of Scurvy Sam, and he shivered. Would Sam be searching for him?

The girl-child tugged his arm. "Old Ma never meant no harm. We got to eat same as other folks." She turned away and pounded the mud with her stick. Large globules of mud splattered her face.

Edwin staggered up from the mud and placed a hand on her shoulder. It was like touching a skeleton. The child squinted up at him.

"What do you want? There won't be no supper for me and old Ma, if' we don't find nofink."

"I'm looking for two chimney sweep boys."

"Don't know none."

Although desperate to leave the stinking mud, Edwin remained. He felt sorry for the child and wanted to help her. "Do you sell what you find?" he asked.

"What do you fink!" She bunched her fist at him.

Edwin grabbed her wrist. He unplugged her from the mud in a single movement, then ran with her on his hip to the wharf steps and set her down.

"Tell me…" he said, panting from the effort, "Tell me what you need to find for one penny."

"5lbs of iron, bones 3lb, rags 2lbs – that's if we can dry 'em. Copper nails." She nodded at him, a happy look on her face. "We gets 4 pence for 1lb weight."

While the child talked, Edwin wormed the remaining silver penny from the toe of his stocking. It wasn't easy with the stocking stiff with mud.

"Take this," he said.

She jumped up and snatched it from his hand. She bit hard on the coin, then her eyes glinted with suspicion. "What do you want for it?"

"Information," said Edwin, focusing on his task again. "Sit down and stop jumping about. I'll say a few names. You nod if you know anyone."

She nodded energetically, her left cheek bulging where she had placed the penny. Edwin described Smudge and then Jake, but the child stared ahead blankly sucking her coin. Similarly, there was no response to the name Carter. Then Edwin remembered Jake saying, 'Bad Bess will have it off you.'

"Bess, Bad Bess," he said, finally.

She spat out the coin and rewarded him with stretched lips. Edwin winced, the smile made her thin little face even uglier.

"I knows of Bad Bess." His heart raced and he clamped a hand to his mouth, trying to appear calm. "It were back awhile. Me Gandfer wished to wed 'er mother. Only he never did." She looked pointedly at his stocking.

Edwin pretended not to notice. Instead, he gazed at the Thames. The river was busy with small craft. Further out, two coal riggers were off-loading into lighter boats. In the short time they'd been on the steps the mist had lifted exposing their foremost sails. He banished the memory of burning sails and turned to the child.

"Explain about Bad Bess."

"I were going to!" She pouted at him, turning sulky. "She were daughter to Ruth, the chimbley sweep. Had 'er own sign she did. Sign of the Woman Chimbly Sweeper, down Nutner's lane."

Edwin jumped up.

"Wait!" The child tugged at his muddy breeches, "She ain't there now." Edwin sat again and she continued. "Ruth went an' wed Jack Jackson and broke me Grandfer's heart. Me Grandfer were a lighterman wiv Jack, and he'd always fancied Ruth.

Anyways, when Jack was took away wiv fever, me grandfer asked her to wed him. But by then Ruth 'ad her own chimbley sweeping business and didn't want no bloke. Now 'er daughter Bad Bess has got it."

Edwin was just about to thank her when she suddenly giggled. "Bess is that bad even the sewer rats be scared."

"Is she married?"

She nodded, "Little gent. A foreigner I fink. Come over on a boat, so Grandfer said."

"Is your grandfather still alive?"

The child leaned close and whispered, "Don't tell me old Grandma." Edwin assured her he wouldn't. "Only she finks he took to sea and is drowned. But I sees him sometimes, up Billingsgate. Don't know where he lives though."

Edwin smiled and got to his feet.

She held up the coin. "Thanks, mister. If I can do anyfink else…"

He left her gazing after him on the Wapping steps.

Chapter 8
Hope

Beyond the Custom House, Billingsgate was alive with gulls. They circled and dive-bombed the quayside, seeking fish guts. Edwin watched where he trod. Eyes of dead fish cobbled the ground. Many of the eyes were white and staring. But others bore dark marks, scratches made by fisherwomen's hobnailed boots. They reminded him of something. Edwin rubbed a hand across his forehead. A pricking sensation troubled him; a warning that something from the past had resurfaced.

He halted.

And remembered.

The skull and crossbones ring! He'd seen that ring before – Scurvy Sam, the sailor who'd punched him in the face, in the fire at sea. He still had the scar. Edwin fingered the deep curve above his left eyebrow. His knees buckled and he half-turned, expecting to see the big sailor. People surged around, but none resembled Sam.

Edwin pinched himself, hard, to recover his senses. He'd just been through the second worst experience of his life; been knocked out and captured, had practically drowned in a sewer, and nearly been eaten alive by rats! And he was still alive. Only a crazed fool would be frightened by someone who wasn't there!

His enquiries about Carter came to nothing. People looked at him askance and backed away as he approached; even fishwives with red arms and sharpened knives. No wonder, he looked like a walking mud bank! After a thorough dousing at a nearby water-pump, he felt and smelt more human. Even so, with the sky overcast, it was mid-day before his damp shirt and breeches stopped clinging to him, and he heard what he'd hoped to hear.

"Si, si, Antonio Carter. Come. I take you. I know a man. He come soon."

Edwin could have hugged him, and he happily accompanied the friendly Italian along the quayside. They walked past several open fronted warehouses, then round to a small tucked away courtyard at the back. In a shady area, three men sat together at a table. As they approached them, the men stood and greeted his guide with noisy cheers. After much backslapping, all four sat down. On the table, there were two boards with black and white squares. The men were part way through a game on one board. Amid excited Italian chatter, counters were placed on the other board. One man wound up a timepiece. Then there was silence.

Edwin stood apart. Had his guide forgotten about him? Counters moved swiftly across the boards and the timepiece ticked loudly. As he waited for the game to finish, Edwin scrutinised each face, and the clothes they were wearing. None of them showed any sign of being a chimney sweep. He tried to catch the eye of his guide, but the Italian was too intent on his game.

The timepiece *pinged* and his guide and opponent shook hands. Edwin had no idea who'd won. At that moment, a tall man entered the yard. He carried the leather cap and protective shoulder wear of a coal heaver. Past middle age, the man was slim, with a long face and sinewy body. He reminded Edwin of somebody. The Italian beckoned him over and introduced him.

"If I can be of any assistance, then Wills is the name." A pleasant smile accompanied his words, and he held out a coal-blackened hand. Edwin did likewise. Wills crushed his hand in an enthusiastic shake. Edwin tried not to wince. He turned to thank his guide but the Italian was engrossed in a second game.

As they left the yard together, Edwin asked if he knew Mr Carter.

"Antonio will not want a lad of your sort," Wills informed him.

Edwin halted. He'd not come this far to be intimidated. He folded his arms and stared the older man in the face, "I'll be the judge of that," he said.

"Ho, Ho!" Wills's face creased up in laughter and he kicked a leg in the air. Edwin pressed his lips together.

"Well I'll tell you what, lad, I'll stop here awhile and light up my pipe, and you can have a think about why you wanted to see me." They stopped in a quiet alleyway and Wills removed a clay pipe from his pocket.

Something soft brushed up against Edwin. He glanced down. A small ginger cat had entwined itself round his leg. The creature was little more than a kitten. He bent down and picked it up. The cat purred.

Wills leaned against the wall, quietly puffing. Smoke circles spiralled upwards from his pipe.

Although much older, there was something about him that reminded Edwin of Jake. He decided to trust him. "I've left home," he said. "And I'm seeking two boys who work for Master Sweep Carter."

"Your folks know where you are?"

"No." The kitten turned and bit his finger. Edwin let it go. It bolted away, disappearing into an open doorway further down the alley, its thin tail held high.

"Bit of an adventure, is it?"

"I have an interest in the trade and wish to know more about it." He kept his voice steady then clamped his mouth shut. He'd said enough. Wills sighed and tapped his pipe out on the wall. Edwin watched the hot ash fall to the cobbles.

"Look, lad, much as I honour the lady, I have to warn you, Antonio keeps well away. Bess Carter owns the business and she's not to be trifled with. She's got four apprentices and she's tough, lad, tough as they come." Wills stressed each word with a prod of his pipe to Edwin's chest. But his softened voice and sly smile conveyed more.

Edwin caught his breath. His heart raced. "Can you get me to the boys without her knowing?" He asked.

"Aye, if we wait for nightfall."

Chapter 9
Carter's Boys

Edwin, having agreed to help the coal heaver, spent much of the afternoon shovelling coal from the wharf into a handcart. He knew he was slow, but Wills seemed pleased enough with his efforts to treat him to pie and ale in the Red Lion. Loaded with coal they set out on their rounds. By nightfall Edwin had lost count of the number of deliveries they'd made. His memory was good for other things, however, and he kept his ears alert for information that might be useful. So far, he'd discovered there were other workers in the trade known as coal-shed men.

"They get up to twenty tons at a time from the coal merchants, and then retail them from a quarter cwt upwards," Wills informed him. He aspired to be one himself, he said, adding, "Competition is great, there being two or three in every low neighbourhood in the city."

Eventually, with Edwin too worn out to take another step, they reached the premises of Bess Carter at number three Swallow Street. It was their last delivery. Wills lifted the coal-hatch lid in the pavement and Edwin stood to one side as he shovelled coal down the coalhole. When he'd finished, he gave Edwin a friendly wink and departed.

Edwin watched the coal heaver until he disappeared with his handcart. There was no one else about. He was on his own now. He moved closer to the coalhole and peered down. Coal was piled high on one side right to the top, propping the lid open. Black lumps glistened in the lamplight. His stomach tightened at the thought of descending into the swirling coal-dust below. It looked scary! Wills had told him the climbing boys lived in the cellar. That gave him courage; that and the fact Smudge should be there and he'd find out about his medallion.

Edwin covered his mouth and nose with his hand and lowered himself into the hole. His weight shifted the heap, and he slid with a cascade of coal straight into Bess Carter's cellar. The coal-hatch lid slammed above him.

As he rose from the coal, Edwin heard gasps from the darkness. The coal-dust settled and pin-pricks of white appeared. He saw four pairs of eyes – two pairs ahead and two beyond the coal heap.

"Blimey! It's Ed!" Smudge recovered first. From somewhere in the shadows he hurled himself at Edwin and pummelled him with his fists. Half in defence, half in elation and relief, Edwin punched him back. A kick to the shins from Jake brought them both to their senses.

"Leave off, Jake. Don't 'yer recognise 'im? It's that young toff what… Aw!" A stinging smack sent Smudge reeling.

Jake glared at Edwin, his eyes glinting with suspicion.

Edwin sensed the older boy's dilemma. And he held out his hand hoping Jake would take it. Jake backed away.

A young voice sang out to him. "I'm Pete. Joe and me, we live here. Have you come to stay?"

"Lay still, Pete, and stop your chatter." The command came from the darkness as a muffled whisper.

Smudge quickly recovered. He pulled Edwin to his corner of the cellar and pushed him down on some sacking. After a growled threat, they'd get the strap if he didn't get some sleep, Jake also retired.

"What you done with yourself?" Smudge asked, wrinkling his nose. "Fall'd down a cess pit!"

Edwin didn't answer, although he might well have done. His own nostrils quivered with unfamiliar smells. He stared into the darker parts of the cellar. As far as he could make out, the section of cellar he was in appeared divided by a line of sacks. The upended sacks bulged with soot. Jake had disappeared behind them. Must be Jake's quarters, he decided. There were plenty of sacks, but he could see no furniture and the coal heap obscured the space beyond.

He gave Smudge a nudge, and whispered, "Who's over there?"

"Joe and Pete. Young un's not well. He's not fit fer the job. Lest-ways, that's what I reckon." Smudge wrapped himself in a sack and closed his eyes.

Edwin was left wondering. Not for long, he wanted answers. He leaned close to the climbing boy's face.

"Smudge, why did you go and leave me?"

"Because," Smudge muttered not opening his eyes.

Edwin shook him. Smudge's eyes flicked open. "Did you take my medallion? I've got to know."

Smudge sat up. "What's a med'lon? Ain't took nothink, Ed." He lay down and turned over.

Edwin smiled to himself and stretched out on the sacking, content to be there. Smudge's friendly welcome gave him a warm happy feeling. He believed Smudge, and he didn't need a medallion to remember his parents; they would always be part of him.

When he woke the following morning, it was still early. The cellar was light enough to read by, or would have been, if he'd had any books. The boys were still sleeping. He could tell by their soft grunts and whistles of breath. As for Smudge, he'd disappeared inside his sack.

A carriage rumbled overhead churning up the street dust. Another bright day with no rain, thought Edwin, watching dust fragments filter down on a sunbeam through the coal-hatch. He remembered his mother telling him they were 'dust devils.'

He heard voices. Moving quietly across to the coal-heap he crouched and listened. Above him, a man and woman were talking in the street close to the hatch. Edwin recognised the man's voice.

"And what would you say if I did admit to it?" The coal heaver's voice sounded low and teasing.

The response was a sniff followed by what Edwin took to be a snigger.

"C'mon, Bessie, it's been months. He's of age."

"And you'll be telling him, will you? Then taking him off me. What'll I do then?" The voice was bright with husky overtones. "Who's to pay? That's what I want to know."

"Now, now, Bess lass. You know you owe me."

Edwin lost interest in the conversation. Someone was watching him. Across the coal-heap an intense pair of eyes held his gaze. He felt unnerved and didn't want to start a conversation. The boy turned away.

Edwin waited a few minutes then moved round the coal - heap to investigate. On the far side of the cellar there were sleeping arrangements for two beds. Some effort had gone into making them comfortable. The little boy was lying on a straw-filled pallet with his head cushioned by a patterned scarf. He slept fitfully, his limbs twitching. His companion, a slim older boy, sat erect and cross-legged on a similar straw pallet. As he came near the boy sprang to his feet with a bunched fist, warning him away.

"Is little Pete your brother?" Edwin spoke quietly. He didn't want to alarm him. The boy nodded fiercely. "Is something wrong with him?"

The boy's eyes filled with tears. He lay down beside Pete and stretched a protective arm across him.

Edwin flushed and moved away, annoyed with himself for asking. The child was obviously ill.

Ponderous footsteps descended the cellar stairs.

Edwin dashed to the coal-heap. The cellar door banged back on its hinges and a husky female voice reverberated round the cellar.

"Get up, you good for nothing lay-abouts!"

It was the same voice he'd heard from the street earlier, only it didn't sound friendly! In the general commotion which followed Edwin buried himself in the coal- heap.

Bess Carter stood in the doorway. As she shouted orders her large frame blocked light from the steps behind her.

Her four apprentices stood to attention in front of her; little Pete rubbing his eyes, struggling to remain upright; Smudge, with a fixed grin; Jake thin and ungainly his neck forward trying to follow his mistress's rambling instructions, and Joe. Edwin noticed that the boy he'd upset was taller than Smudge and the set of his head on a long slim neck gave him a graceful appearance.

Joe spoke first. "My brother is unfit. I beg you, mistress, let…"

"You'll do as you're told," interrupted Jake. "Mistress Carter will give the boy some broth and he'll soon recover. Isn't that so, Mistress?"

"Well, Jake, it's up to you, now. You're foreman. If he can't work, there's plenty can."

Little Pete let out a cry and crumpled to the floor.

Bess Carter ignored him. "Make that Northumberland Terrace, numbers one to sixteen and no piking!" There was one more command, "And shift that coal before you go."

The door slammed behind her. There was silence. Edwin heard her heavy breathing as she mounted the steps.

"'Bout time she 'ad a heart attack," Smudge said, cheerfully.

While hiding in the coal heap, Edwin had time to study Bess Carter. The mud lark girl had described her as frightening. She was grossly overweight, he couldn't deny that, and the pits and scars of small pox covered her face. Yet there was something about her. Her plumpness was distributed in curves and with her dark glossy hair and tall frame, he could imagine her once attractive.

Thinking about it; most of the women in his life were attractive, well-dressed ladies; women like his mother and aunts, who could afford to look their best. An image of his cousin Mary, rosy cheeked and sophisticated loomed before him. His eyes snapped shut; what would she think if she saw him now!

Edwin clambered out of the coal-heap and brushed himself down. When he looked up, he was surprised to see Jake carrying Pete to his straw pallet.

The little boy spotted him and sang out, "Good morning, Mr Coalman."

"Well enough to speak then are you?" Jake said, dumping him down.

"I can sift the soot, Jake. Pass me a sack and I'll do it, honest."

Joe intervened. "He could, Jake. It's only his legs. He can manage if he doesn't have to stand or climb."

Edwin stared round the cellar. He had no idea what they were talking about until he noticed a large pile of lumpy-looking soot.

"There's more 'n four sacks." Jake sounded unconvinced.

"Well I can help him," said Joe.

"He'll have to do it on his own. You've gotta come with us."

"I-am-not-leaving-Pete!" Joe stamped the floor.

Edwin pushed between them, "Why can't you take me? I've been up a chimney. I'd like to help."

Jake moved across to his quarters and returned with two shovels.

"If you're fit after shifting that lot," he said, indicating the coal-heap, "I'll think about it." He opened the cellar door and left them to it.

"If we work fast," Smudge said, "There'll be time for you to practise on St George's."

"Oooo," squealed little Pete, clapping his hands, "I'd like to see the coalman climb the wall!"

"What wall?" Edwin asked.

"The church wall what I'll have t' teach you to climb, Booby! It's not so bad." Smudge grinned, "So long as you don't get piked on a spike! 'Course you got to fall on to one first." Smudge seemed to think this hilarious and laughed until tears streaked his sooty face.

Pete squealed again, and even Joe grinned.

Was Smudge being serious? Edwin glared at him. No time to find out. Jake had returned with six large baskets for the coal.

As he helped Smudge fill the baskets, Edwin tried not to think about his hands, still sore from yesterday's shovelling. He looked across at Joe and Pete and asked about the soot.

"We have t' sift it, to get all the lumps out. Mistress sells best soot—"

"To the wheat farmers," interrupted Edwin. Smudge punched him, impressed.

Jake helped carry the loaded baskets of coal up the cellar steps. As he stacked them in the hall he kept glancing up the stairs to the upper rooms. Edwin guessed he was looking out for Bess, while he hopped it with Smudge through the front door.

It was a relief to get outside. He wondered when they'd get anything to eat, but he felt happy accompanying Smudge and Jake up the street. He'd made friends, he was learning about life, and about to do something useful. Sweeping chimneys couldn't be that difficult! He looked back at number three Swallow Street. Bess Carter's house was two stories high and narrow, one in a terrace of houses, all with attics. He stopped and studied the roof top. He counted three pairs of chimney pots, six in all. They were close together on a large central chimney stack.

"If you're counting pots," Smudge stood at his side, "What you got to remember—" Jake shouted at them to get a move on. They ignored him.

Smudge pointed up at the roofs. "Three pots fer Carter, number three, means, three fireplaces each wiv a flue an' a pot. Then three pots wiv the same fer number four, next door. Party walls, see, wiv fireplaces back t' back."

Edwin puzzled this out as they carried on up the street. He'd seen little of the interior of Bess Carter's house. The stairs from the cellar had led up to a narrow hall with a parlour to one side, and there must be a kitchen at the back. The bedroom above must have a fireplace.

Jake stayed with them until they reached Major Foubert's riding school on the street corner. By the time they'd turned into George Street, Jake had disappeared.

"He'll be looking at the nags," Smudge told him. "Though I don't s'ppose you'd call 'em nags. Nor do Jake. They be proper horses, fer gents like you." Then a thought seemed to strike him. "Ed, carry on down to St George's Church. Jus' follow the railings, an' wait fer me." Smudge left him and bolted back around the corner.

As Edwin followed the iron railings round to the front of St George's he tried not to notice their pointed spikes. Milkmaids and costermongers were out and about, shouting for trade. He felt horribly exposed, and darted up the church steps to the porch, thankful for its deep shadow.

The great arched door of the church was closed. Edwin pressed his cheek to the knotted wood. Inside, he heard the throbbing sounds of an organ. Or was it his own heart pounding! A pain gripped his stomach. Was he scared of the climb? Or maybe the familiar sound of the organ was luring him back to the Abbey School? He screwed up his eyes and thumped his head on the door.

"You goin' crazy?"

Smudge seized his arm and pulled him away. "Here, get some food in you." Smudge thrust two crinkled yellow apples into his hand.

The flesh tasted sweet and spongy; he hadn't eaten properly for days. That's what it was, hunger, making him lightheaded. "Where did you get them?" he asked, gulping down another mouthful.

"Back of the riding school. They store 'em there, fer the nags." Smudge watched as he sank his teeth into the second apple. "I took some time choosing those."

"I… I'm sorry, have you—"

"Course I 'ave! Gorged myself proper afore I got 'em fer you."

Minutes later, Edwin was ready to face his challenge. He stood inside the railings at the corner of the church.

"Up you go," said Smudge, pushing him close to the wall.

He gazed slowly upwards. Between the great blocks of projecting stone were narrow grooves. The blocks rose up the corner of the building to the hazy blue of the sky. They swam before his eyes….

"Don't think." Smudge grabbed his hand and pushed his fingers in a groove. "Jus' keep goin' up. I'll be right behind yer."

Determined to show he could do it, and not let Smudge see how terrified he was, Edwin started to climb.

He could feel Smudge's presence behind him, urging him on, and shouting encouragement: "Arm up to the right… now right toe; left arm up… keep flat, keep flat… There's a juicy lamb chop at the top!"

As his arms got used to the strain, he established a rhythm. If he stopped now, he'd fall. The only way was up – and grip – and pull, grip and pull. He stopped and glanced upwards. From the flatness of the wall and the angle he was at, he couldn't see the top! Sweat ran down his face into his eyes. He squeezed them tight, then opened them again and looked down. Smudge had vanished. Immediately below him, the railing tops pointed straight up at him. He stared at them, his eyes bulging. A chill crept up his spine. Impaled on one of the spikes was a piece of orange peel. Test of sharpness? Dropped by a passing bird – Or! Edwin made up his mind. Safer to climb down, confess that he'd failed, or pretend, perhaps, that he had done it. He'd decide later.

Edwin lifted his foot from the wall, slid his leg down to the grove below....

"Another few yards. C'mon Ed. I'm up here." A voice from the roof. "Keep looking up. You can do it." Smudge's face, grinning down at him. The climbing boy's cheery voice continued – until he got going again. And he didn't stop. And somehow...

FINALLY!

He reached Smudge's helping hand at the top. Wasting no time – the constables would be after them if spotted – they slid together down the tiles and over the guttering to the outhouse roof below. Then a climb down the waste pipe to the ground. It was obvious now, how Smudge had got to the roof.

They stood and grinned at each other,

"It's a good life, Ed."

"You could have killed me!"

"We all done it. Mistress made us. We couldn't work fer 'er else." Smudge grinned and wagged a grimy finger. "It was you what wanted to be a chummy!"

Edwin ginned back, he could forgive Smudge anything.

Chapter 10
A Shock for Mary

Mary's family were doing their best to find Edwin. An urgent message had been dispatched to Lord Robert at sea, and her father had persuaded his sister-in-law, Elizabeth, to place an advert in the *Daily Register*. Everyone hoped that an offer of £20 reward would bring news.

Even so, Mary was desperate to do something positive again. Should she confess, she wondered, tell her parents she'd visited a derelict cottage unescorted and found Edwin's medallion? Whether she did not it wouldn't help find her cousin, and she'd get herself and Amos into trouble. It was a dilemma. When she heard that one of the horses at Major Floubert's riding school had fallen lame she offered to help out with her pony. A good excuse to be absent from her mother's bedside, she reasoned, and more important, she could explore a different part of London. Besides, Rats would appreciate the attention.

"You'll enjoy the exercise," she told her pony, patting Rats's plump belly, "And while you're there, you behave yourself!" She ignored her father's concern about unrest in the city and set off alone to Major Floubert's riding school.

Again, she failed to consider Rats's feelings and the strong-willed pony rebelled. He even refused an offer of last season's apples, and a disgruntled Mary led a victorious Rats away from the riding stables. Mary won in the end. She knew Rats looked forward to a good canter, and she punished him by walking.

They were trotting up the New Road towards Marylebone Park when Mary noticed a tall lanky boy ambling along in front of them. He walked with a slight limp and kept glancing back at

Rats. When they drew level, the boy moved close to her pony and patted his flank. Rats appeared happy about this and blew down his nose.

Mary glared at the boy; though she saw now, he was older than she'd thought. About sixteen, she decided. He took no notice of her, only having eyes for Rats.

A gang of noisy costermongers suddenly interrupted them. They were carrying banners and notices on wooden boards with the wording: STOP THE BILL.

"No Popery! No Popery!" The Catholic haters shouted, surging around them. The pony whinnied and stamped the ground. The boy shouted at them, to clear the way. They parted. And there, in front of her laughing and shoving each other off the sidewalk, were two scruffy-looking boys. One was slightly taller and his clothes less ingrained in soot. His face....

Mary dropped the reins.

Her eyes widened in disbelief. It was her cousin, and she'd barely recognised him! Edwin stood rooted to the pavement. For a second Mary was struck as dumb as he was, then she recovered herself.

"Ed... w in!" she gasped.

Smudge rushed forward, babbling to Jake, telling him about Ed climbing the church wall.

Edwin stepped forward. He grabbed a handful of Smudge's ragged sleeve and pushed him towards her. "Mary," he said. She heard the strangled emotion in his voice. "Meet my friend, Smudge. He's a climbing boy."

Smudge glanced from her back to Edwin and he scratched his head. "She don't look too happy," he said.

"No, no... I... Pleased to meet you, Smudge."

"Likewise, Miss."

"I'm his foreman, Jake," announced Jake. "And we're pleased to make your acquaintance." He nuzzled his head against her pony's shoulder.

Mary grabbed the reins. She creased her brow, staring hard at Edwin pleading with him for some kind of explanation, but he hurried past, giving Rats a casual glance as he went.

"Steady there. Look after your mistress," he muttered.

Smudge gave her a mock salute.

Mary stayed rigid, glaring after the two boys, willing Edwin to turn round. Surely, he wouldn't leave her like that? Walk past her with no explanation when they'd always been friends! A lump came to her throat. What had happened to him?

He didn't glance back. Then they were out of sight. And good riddance too, she thought, dashing a furious tear from her eye.

"Some kin of yours, is he, Miss?" She'd forgotten about Jake. "I'll fetch him back, if that's what you want."

"No," she shouted, and she swung herself up to the sidesaddle. "I want nothing to do with him." She couldn't wait to get away, be on her own to yell and scream her frustration.

Rats gathered his hooves and cantered away.

No time to think about Mary. The street Edwin and Smudge were in was crowded with foot soldiers. News had spread fast that protesters were heading for parliament. Expecting a riot, troops had been called. They spilled into the carriageway. Sheer force of numbers displaced sellers of wares, forcing beggars and fashionable folk alike into the path of carriages.

Edwin stood close to Smudge on the sidewalk, wary of flying hooves and clattering wagon wheels, watching, waiting for a break in the general pandemonium. A brewer's dray halted in front of them. Smudge seized the opportunity and pushed him forward. When the dray moved on, both he and Smudge were settled on the low tailboard.

"Where's it going?" Edwin asked.

"To the Turk's Head, but it'll do us alright. Jump when I say." Smudge chuckled, "Things be warming up sure 'nough."

Edwin suspected that Smudge knew less about politics than he did. As the dray's two horses sped past Charing Cross, Edwin swivelled and bounced on his bottom. Fresh horse dung splattered his feet. The barrels of ale behind him bruised his spine and there was nothing to hang on to.

"L—ean—b—ack—an… hug your—n, knees," Smudge shouted jerking up and down.

Somehow, they stayed on until Smudge yelled: "Now!" and they leapt from the dray to the parched yellow grass of St James's Park.

Smudge sprang to his feet. "We're heading over there," he said, pointing to the far side of the park.

Before he scooted off, Edwin grabbed his ankle. Smudge pitched forward, and Edwin pinned him down. "Keep still or I'll punch your monkey-face," he threatened, raising his fist.

Smudge stopped struggling. Edwin leant over him, bringing his face close "You're not going anywhere until I get some answers!"

"Phew, Ed! You had me right worrit." Smudge tried to sit up, but Edwin pressed a knee to his chest. The climbing boy started panting, "There's work to do; chimbleys what want coring... lumme, Ed, git off, an' then I can tell yer!"

Edwin relaxed his hold. As Smudge wriggled to a sitting position Edwin burst out laughing. Bits of twig and dried grass had attached themselves to his spiky hair; Smudge resembled a disgruntled hedgehog.

Smudge scowled, "You listening or not?" Edwin sobered up and nodded. "We got to climb the chimbley flues in Northumberland Terrace and remove rubble what builders have left behind. Shouldn't take mor'n a few hours." His grin returned. "Monday's best day of the week. We gets most of the day off."

"Why's that?"

"Mistress, and coal heaver Wills, sometimes," Smudge added, grudgingly. "They takes orders on Mondays. Off of the gentry mostly. 'Course season's slack now, being summer, though me an' Jake knows ways round it." He tapped the side of his nose; his meaning clear.

Edwin frowned, "Against the law!"

"Course it's alright fer you toffs with your servants and banquets. You wouldn't know about the likes of us!" Smudge leapt up, bristling. He cupped his hands to his mouth and yelled,

"Rights to the people. Down with Papists!"

A party of gentlefolk strolling nearby pretended not to notice. Further away, a rat seller and several street cleaners took up the cry.

Smudge plonked himself down again. "Embarrass your Lordship, did I?"

"I know more than you think, braggart!" Edwin out stared him. "Remember that court case at the Old Bailey last year, against stamp duty on hay sold at Smithfield?" Smudge looked bored and closed his eyes. "My uncle put up the money," he shouted in Smudge's ear, "For the defence!"

Before Smudge retaliated, Edwin got to his feet and set off across the park.

Later, in the basement of Number one Northumberland Terrace, Edwin was less sure of himself. He faced the boiler flue. It looked narrow and uninviting. There were butterflies in his stomach and he wished he was back in the park.

"Forget about easy climbs, Ed." Smudge pushed him forward. "Up you go. I'll be right behind yer, like afore."

Smudge knelt down in the fireplace. Edwin kicked off his canvas shoes and climbed on to Smudge's shoulders. As his head entered the flue, he smelt the pungent reek of fresh mortar.

"Get a move on, or I'll nibble yer toes," Smudge promised, staggering upright again.

Edwin didn't doubt he would. As he forced himself to climb, he felt Smudge's breath hot on his feet. Above him, the sloping shoulder of the flue narrowed and continued upwards. He remembered that flues travelled up several storeys through chimneys in terraced houses. He saw no daylight and had to feel with his fingers for craggy holds.

"Ouch!" He stifled another cry... Smudge might hear him and think him a sissy! His body was too large to pull away from the sides of the flue, there was nothing for it, but bear the pain and ignore the brickwork chaffing his elbows and knees as he pushed upwards. Sweat trickled down his face. He rested. It was cold below. Had Smudge left him? How long had he been on his own?

"Smudge!" his throat tightened and only a strangled squeak came out. Think of something... anything... Fire! No. No! The flue was empty; he was in a clean new chimney. Breathe, breathe slowly… Better… Better. Think of Mary. No! His eyes watered. He had to get out!

'Up, Ed.' Smudge's voice in his head, reassuring, 'Get a move on… that's it. Keep goin'….'

Finally, a circle of light. But it darkened over….

"You asleep?" Smudge's face, blocking the pot, peering down at him. How had he got there so quickly?

"I come up the attic flue next door, had to make sure you was all right." Smudge explained, and then instructed him to, "Get back down, then up the flues in the back rooms. That'll be ground, and the next two floors," he said.

"How many flues in each stack?"

"Sixteen, eight fer each house; basement, ground and first floor I already done 'em. When you gets next door, you do the upper rooms, and I'll do the long un's."

Smudge's face swam before him; four eyes, two noses… Heat confused Edwin's brain; he had to get out! He stretched up. Smudge withdrew, and he elongated his body and squeezed through the chimney pot. It was worth the effort. The sun blazed on the roof, but the row of sixteen pots produced their own shade.

While he rested, Smudge snapped a corner off a slate tile. He used the fragment of tile to scrape a diagram on the side of a pot. The pot being terracotta the white outlines were clear. Edwin studied the diagram. Smudge had drawn flues with angles and differing lengths.

"What you got to remember is," said Smudge, "that the longest flue comes from the basement and the shortest from the attic. In this row that'd be numbers one and five."

"This one," said Edwin, leaning back against the pot, "Must serve the second floor."

"You got it, Ed." Smudge grinned and left him to get on with it.

Before descending, he glanced across at the next row of pots. Smudge waved, then disappeared down the first pot of the adjoining house.

It took several hours, with rests, to check his allotted flues. Apart from removing small amounts of rubble in some of the bends, the main job was dislodging newly built birds' nests. While climbing he'd surprised a sitting jay and annoyed several starlings. Smudge's drawing of flues helped. Visualising the angle and judging how far to climb kept him going.

He'd tried to prove himself by keeping up with Smudge. But experience told and the climbing boy shouted at him to, "Stick to the shorter flues." He did, but almost gave up when faced with the last flue of house number six.

Two storeys of vertical climb…. His exhausted limbs couldn't keep going. Anyway, he told himself, whose to know if I climb the flue or not? And he turned away from the hearth. It was no good; he'd be failing a challenge and letting himself down.

The slow drag up seemed to last forever and there was nothing to clear.

He rested in the flue, just below the lower bulge of pot. No point in squeezing through. Impossible anyway, his limbs refused. He'd done it, though! Twenty-four flues – some satisfaction in that. The air above smelt musty but comforting. His eye caught a small glint. He shifted. The glint was still there. There was something wedged in the upper rim of the pot.

Edwin stretched up and prized it free. The sun shone on its surface.

It was a silver penny.

Chapter 11
On the Scent

Back home again, Mary entered her mother's bedchamber and stopped, astonished. Charlotte, her normally languid parent was sitting on the edge of her bed looking bright eyed and cheerful.

Her mother smiled and stretched out her arms, "Help me up, Mary," she said. "I've rung for the maid. I shall have my hair brushed and get dressed for dinner."

Mary hurried to fetch her mother's slippers. She supported her with an arm round her waist as Charlotte took a few faltering steps across the floor. Her mother's small white feet shone like pearls in the slippers. Upturned at the toes and made of rich blue brocade, they'd arrived from Turkey years ago as a Christmas present from Edwin's mother.

"Your mind is elsewhere, Mary!"

She'd not heard a word of her mother's breathless chatter. "I'm sorry, Mama," she said, settling her mother in a wicker chair beside the dressing table.

Charlotte caught her hand and clasped it. "Now this is what I want you to do." Mary winced as her hold tightened. "You must visit your Aunt Elizabeth. Go immediately, Mary." Her mother spoke with passion. "Your uncle is still at sea, and probably unaware of the dreadful circumstances. Dear Elizabeth must be beside herself with worry." Her mother's eyes watered.

Mary looked away. She daren't say what she was thinking. Her mother and her Aunt Elizabeth were fond of one another, but they put on a front when together and never showed their true feelings. Neither understood the other at all.

"Your father has taken it upon himself," her mother was saying, "to place a second advert; this time in the *Universal News*. Two sources of information being better than one, and with a more substantial reward, Mary. Imagine that!" Charlotte's brow furrowed. "Edwin's been missing for days. What would my poor dead brother and my sister-in-law have thought of us all? Losing a nephew, and an heir at that! Oh my lord!"

Mary prized her hand free. "Mama, please don't get overexcited. I will go see Aunt Elizabeth. I promise."

The door opened and Charlotte's maid entered. Gwyneth was a country girl, whose name her mother never remembered. She gave them both a quick bob and picked up her mistress's silver-handled hairbrush. As Mary watched her lift and brush her mother's long copper tresses, it seemed a good moment to say what she'd been steeling herself to say.

"Mama, before I go," Mary began, tentatively, "I want to ask you if... If you know..." She almost lost her nerve, and finished in a rush, "Any chimney sweeps?"

Charlotte jerked away from the brushes. "Know any chimney sweeps! Pray, what makes you think *I* could be acquainted with any chimney sweeps?"

"Know the names of any, I mean." Her mother stared at her as though she'd gone insane. "Mama, we do have our chimneys swept!"

"And do you suppose that is any concern of mine?" A hard edge had crept into her mother's voice.

Mary swung away, her emotions topsy-turvy. Edwin had been on her mind since meeting him the previous day and been too shocked to do anything; still furious with him, she'd be on his side whatever happened. She gripped her hands together until the knuckles whitened, agonising about whether to tell her mother.

"Well, I do know one, Miss Mary." Mary turned. "Antonio Carter," said Gwyneth, coming up to her. "He was a Master Sweep. He was friendly with that oyster seller, the one what now owns the Chandlers. They used to meet up reg'lar."

Mary moved silently, "Where?"

"Fishing, down in the Fleet River." Gwyneth went back to her brushing.

Charlotte closed her eyes with a sigh.

Mary thanked the maid. She gave her mother a brief, 'no hard feelings' kiss on the cheek and slipped from the room.

The name of any sweep was better than none, she decided, hurrying outside. She had to find him again and make him return, or, or, she didn't want to consider the consequences. Oh, Edwin, she murmured to herself. What are you doing? They'll never forgive you if they find out who you're with.

As she approached Rats's stables, an image of a child with soot-encrusted ears swam before her. Her mind cleared. And she remembered the little boy and his brother, walking away hand-in-hand to sweep chimney flues. The flues of wealthy people, like her parents. Flues swept several times a year, with no one caring about the children who climbed them. Her eyes filled with tears. What a dreadful life they must lead.

Edwin was savouring a large hot spiced-gingerbread, bought on the street with his penny. He ate quickly, cramming it into his mouth. But Mary was uppermost in his mind and the more he remembered, the slower he munched.

What must she think of him? Seeing her like that with her pony in the street, he'd almost died of embarrassment. His clothes were in a dreadful state and he'd not washed for days. She'd even recognised him! At least he'd had the good manners to introduce Smudge and Jake. She'd responded so well. His face burned. The gingerbread crumbled in his hand. There was a fluttering of wings and chirping, and open-beaked sparrows gathered at his feet. Edwin threw them the crumbs.

He ached all over and his knees throbbed. Best think about something else, and he remembered the river.

When he got there, Edwin plunged into the water, fully clothed. He'd always been a strong swimmer, and the tide was with him, flowing up stream. Unlike his terrifying swoosh down the sewer, he was in control and decide when and where to stop. Such luxury; lying in the swell of the river, floating face up watching the darkening sky, drifting just beyond the trailing willows and the bank.

A secluded break in the reeds appeared. Edwin rolled over and swam towards the bank. As he emerged from the river streaming with water, a lone fisherman shouted out to him.

"Salute! A Neptune arises!"

Edwin was tempted to reply to the little man with a suitable Latin text. Instead, he extended his hand and apologised for disturbing his fishing.

"No fish today," he replied in a strong accent. "Fish too lazy, no lika zee heat. Me, I lika zee heat."

Edwin stood shivering in front of him. It was early evening and the sun had sunk well below the horizon. "So do I. Es-sspecially now," Edwin replied through chattering teeth.

The friendly man handed Edwin a roll of sacking he'd been using as a headrest.

"Thank you, sir. I'm very grateful." Edwin shook out the sacking and removed some of his clothes. While he dried himself, he turned his back on the fisherman, not wanting him to see the exposed sores on his elbows and knees.

The little Italian's keen eyes took everything in. His tongue stayed silent, however, and he returned to his fishing line and settled down again.

Instead of handing back the sack and leaving, Edwin stayed. Something attracted him to the friendly man with his strong foreign accent. Italian, Edwin guessed, remembering a part of Northern Italy he'd visited with his parents when young. It had been on one of their rare trips back from England when his father had been with them.

"May I sit down with you, sir?" Edwin asked. He'd only been away a few days, but he felt a sudden need for intellectual conversation. The stranger, he sensed, was a kindred spirit; unsurprising, given his knowledge of Latin.

There was no hesitation in the fisherman's voice when he replied. "But yes. Ze reeds, all ze river reeds are free. I come, I sit and I dream…."

"Of anything in particular, sir?"

"Of Italy. Always of Italy."

Edwin lay back beside him. He agreed with the Italian. The reeds, waving in the river breeze above and around them were conducive to dreaming, and the two of them remained in friendly silence.

Then his new companion turned to him and smiled. He was ready to talk. Edwin heard about his Italian childhood. How he'd spent hours clambering up and down the craggy mountain slopes of his hillside village. Water had to be brought from the river below, often several times a day. And it was the agility of youngsters like him that turned the poor children of Piedmont into the roaming chimney sweeps of Europe.

Edwin sat up. The children's expertise was highly sort after, the Italian told him. At least Edwin guessed that was what he meant to say with his muddled English phrasing. And he explained that many had made their way across the sea to England, including him.

"I lucky, I marry English girl with business. My Italian family here find her for me. How you say it – marriage of zee—"

"Marriage of convenience."

The Italian beamed, "Si, but I have to take her name." His face took on a woeful look. "I not have business no more. My Bess, my belissima girl, she drink too much. She no so nice now and she have new man in her life."

Edwin could think of nothing cheerful to say. So they sat gazing at the river. A swarm of tiny insects emerged from the reeds, spiralled into the air, then descended and settled elsewhere, out of sight. On mass and together, Edwin thought with a pang of envy.

"Do you get used to being on your own?" he blurted out.

The Italian got to his feet. "I am not on my own. I have all of zis," he said waving his arms and grinning at Edwin, as though declaring ownership of a vast estate.

Edwin looked away, mortified. It struck him that here he was, heir to his uncle's estate, and he did nothing but moan! He sprang up, determined to get on with the challenge of proving himself. He'd started well and already made friends. This was apparent when the Italian clasped his hands and pumped them up and down in a fond farewell. Now they were standing upright and close to each other, they were the same height. The Italian had stooped shoulders. Edwin judged him to be about sixty years old. With dark craggy eyebrows and springy greying hair, he somewhat resembled a goat. Edwin grinned, he could imagine him leaping from rock to rock down a mountain slope.

Realising that his new friend was about to leave and he may never see him again, Edwin asked him his name.

"Antonio," he called back, waving his fishing rod above the reeds.

Edwin frowned. Could he be...? He thought for a few minutes, then decided to follow Antonio back to where he lived hoping what he suspected, wouldn't turn out to be true.

Mary just missed seeing Edwin.

She'd set off on Rats and followed the towpath beside the river, all the way from the New River Head, London's new water supply, when the path disappeared and she had to coax Rats through acres of reeds. She determined not to miss a single stretch. The riverbank was popular with fishermen, and she remembered Joe and Pete swam in the river to get clean; two compelling links with sweeps. Unfortunately, while pushing through reeds, a plague of insects decided to settle on Rats.

The pony had planted his feet, flicked his tail, and refused to go any further. Mary, despairing, abandoned her search for Edwin and headed home.

When she arrived, she found events had taken a surprising turn.

Chapter 12
A Good Deed

Edwin raced up the cobbled alleyway, his heart pounding. He'd agreed to meet Smudge on the steps of St Brides at noon. He'd heard the mid-day chimes but taken a detour. Antonio hadn't gone to Swallow Street at all, but turned into Seven Dials and entered a boarding house off Drury Lane. A grim area at the best of times, but *phew*; such a relief he didn't live with Bess. It had been worth finding out. He put on an extra spurt.

St Bride's Church came into view. His heart beat quickened. Would Smudge be there? He lost sight of the church for a minute as a noisy crowd appeared from nowhere and surged towards him. They seemed to be heading south. He skirted around them and saw Smudge, sitting on the church steps, eating.

Edwin plonked down beside him.

"What kept yer?" Smudge bit into a chuck of bread and eyed him suspiciously. "I already done the long flues, up the Admiralty," he said, bits of bread spattering from his mouth. "Right foggy holes, they was." Foggy holes, Edwin made a mental note. "Had to do 'em all on me own. Young Pete were coughin' so bad, Jake sent 'im home."

If Edwin hadn't been bursting with his own news, he would have worried about Pete having to work. But he waited until Smudge finished chewing and told him about meeting Antonio.

"That'll be Carter alright, mistress's old mister. We don't never see anyfink of him. Not now we don't."

"Why's that?"

"Not since she took to drinking gin an' got so fat. She'd make mutton chops of him wiv 'er temper." Smudge chuckled, almost choking at the idea. He stood up. "Come on, stir your stumps. We've got work... he paused, "If you want."

He sounded grudging as though reluctant or having second thoughts. Edwin stood beside him and punched his arm. "Where are we going?" he said.

"Nowhere in partic'lar... Just, testing." Edwin stared at him. No grin on Smudge's face. He couldn't fathom him out. Was he serious?

"It's like this, see, Ed. I've got me itchy feet. An' what wiv the rioters, things be getting worse round here. Its best t' get away." Smudge grinned. "You game then?"

There were many people about and the atmosphere was uneasy. As Edwin hurried along with Smudge, they had to push through crowds on the pavement, and carts came to a standstill as people took to the road. Many, Edwin noticed, armed with bricks and cudgels!"

Smudge knew the quickest routes through back alleys and they soon found themselves alone. At Seven Dials, Edwin glanced round, and stopped.

"Smudge, tell me where you're heading."

"North."

Edwin grabbed his arm. "No. Smudge listen, I can't go north!"

"If you wants t' come wiv me, I'm goin' north. Don't know no other place." He pulled away and walked on.

Edwin stood there, now what? He understood Smudge well enough to believe he'd not change his mind. And why should he? The climbing boy didn't need him, he needed Smudge, to learn the ropes, so to speak; how to be a chummy.

On the outskirts of Camden town, they came across a small group of people. They stood around an abandoned horse and cart. The horse looked as dejected as an old horse could be. His head hung low, and the reins dangled from his neck.

Edwin rushed forward. He'd recognise that cart anywhere. No sign of the farmer, but inside the cart, a large white goose, Blackfoot. Where were the others? Probably sold at market.

"Take the reins, Smudge," he shouted.

Smudge grabbed the horse's reins.

The onlookers comprised women and young children. Edwin turned to a washerwoman with a basket on her hips. "Where's the farmer?" he asked. She opened her mouth to reply, but Blackfoot set up such a commotion of hissing and honking, he barely heard her. As far as he could make out, the farmer had been found unconscious and taken away.

"Does anyone know anything about the farmer?" Edwin addressed the onlookers.

One of the women made way for an elderly man, who hopped towards him. He wore the tatty uniform of an old soldier. He leaned heavily on his crutch and stamped his wooden peg leg down so close to Edwin he almost pronged his foot. His breath smelt of stale ale as he leaned close.

Blackfoot, perhaps sensing an older masculine presence, fell silent.

"He's been took off," muttered the old soldier, "By them who knows where they took him." On imparting this unhelpful information, the old soldier nodded twice. Not waiting for Edwin's response, he turned and hobbled off.

That being settled, the onlookers melted away.

The horse fidgeted and jerked its head from side to side. Edwin spoke to it quietly and stroked it between the ears, something he remembered seeing Amos do with his aunt's mare. It appeared to work. The horse calmed and softly nibbled his wrist with its lips. Complete acceptance, it seemed. Only one thing for it, Edwin decided, he'd have to take responsibility.

Smudge was hopping from foot to foot chortling. Edwin took over the reins, and Smudge clambered up to the front seat whistling and puffing out his cheeks in obvious excitement.

Edwin joined him and flicked the reins. He'd driven a horse and cart before but had no idea where to go. He'd let the horse decide. Consequently, they ambled straight ahead.

"Lummy, Ed," Smudge shouted. "I ain't done nofik like this afore!" Smudge turned to him with eyes shining with admiration. "You done well, Ed."

Edwin grinned. He was happy for Smudge, but wished they weren't heading north to Hertfordshire. So close to home he might be recognised, and he wasn't ready to return. That prickly sensation came again. A premonition something was about to happen.

And it did. As they trotted past the Black Swan Inn, the old horse reared, startled by a sudden noise.

The Inn door had opened and a drunken group of sailors staggered out onto the pavement. Edwin caught a look at them. His heart thumped against his ribs. Surely not! One of them was Scurvy Sam! The big sailor was too drunk to notice him. Edwin slapped the reins on the horse's rump and yelled, "Giddy up!" No qualms now about leaving the city!

"Gee! Nearly came a cropper there, Ed!" Smudge had been frightened by the horse rearing in his face, but it didn't take him long to recover. Excitement over having a horse and cart set him babbling.

"Jake won't never believe what you done. Don't rightly believe it m' self wiv me own eyes, I don't! We're gonna be alright with this little lot, make a mint o' money!"

"Get no funny ideas, Smudge! There's no way this horse and cart, or goose, will stay in our possession." He glared at Smudge, hoping to convince him.

Smudge looked outraged, "I ain't having none of that, Ed! What we got here, is ours. We got possession sure 'nough." He folded his arms, rebellious.

"They don't belong to us!"

"So you tell me who they does belong to."

"The farmer."

Smudge snorted. "What farmer? I don't see no farmer! Where's he at, then? What's his name?" Edwin stared ahead. "You don't know, do yer? Nor where he lives."

He'd hesitated too long; Smudge looked smug.

"I have a fair idea," Edwin said, giving Smudge a studied look. "I've travelled in this cart before, and I know the farmer. Maybe not by name, or where he lives, but I'll find out."

Fate was with him. They had reached a quiet area, where no traffic rumbled past. The horse stopped. He swung his head first one way, and then the other, as though seeking something.

Satisfied, he trotted across the road and turned down a narrow street.

Realising the horse was following his instincts, Edwin let him go. Besides, the street looked familiar. He'd been here before with the farmer. It was where he'd sold his shoes. And sure enough the horse stopped midway down the street, outside the Chandlers.

Smudge clutched his arm. Before Edwin could reassure him, the shop door banged back against its hinges and the owner emerged with a large sack across his shoulders.

"Thought you'd be here before now," he grumbled. "Just about to close up." Edwin threw the reins to a surprised Smudge and jumped down. The chandler chuckled. "Got you working for him now, has he?"

Edwin took the sack from him and nodded. The less said the better.

While Smudge stayed where he was, he helped load two more sacks into the cart. Blackfoot, familiar with the routine, didn't interfere.

Not sure if the chandler expected some kind of payment, Edwin followed him into the shop. The chandler turned back, surprising him, "Sold your shoes," he said lowering his voice to a whisper. It was the way he said it, out of earshot of Smudge, as though he knew him. His neck muscles stiffened. The chandler was waiting; he'd have to say something.

He took a deep breath, "May I ask who bought them?" he said, trying to sound casual.

"That you may, young Sir." Edwin felt himself blushing. There was a deliberate stress on the 'Sir.' "A pretty young lady she was. Very respectful. Gentry, I'd say."

Time to go! Edwin headed for the door, "I hope you got good money for them," he called back.

"Aye, I did," replied the chandler, chuckling.

As Edwin walked the horse to the end of the street and turned the cart, he was thankful for Smudge's silence. Mary, again! Why couldn't she leave him alone! His conscience pricked even thinking about her! Why had she gone to the Chandler's? So many unanswered questions....

He climbed up beside Smudge and took the reins. Clear of the Chandler's shop, he sighed with relief. He'd half expected the man to reappear and extort some kind of blackmail. His relations must be worried by now. Perhaps they'd even offered a reward! He gave himself a shake. Mary had seen him; she would have told them he was safe.

Edwin turned to Smudge, his eyes were closed and his head nodding. He wanted to shake him awake then remembered that Smudge had been up early that morning sweeping foggy holes. He tightened the reins. They'd left the city behind and heading into open countryside with no idea where they were going. It was up to him now; decide what to do… And it came to him. Obvious really. Why hadn't he thought of it before? He pulled the reins. The horse stopped.

Smudge sat up with a jolt. "What's up, where… Where've we got to?"

"Nowhere, yet. Get the goose out, Smudge."

Smudge sucked in his breath and rubbed his stomach. "A bit of goose would go down a treat!"

Edwin laughed. Normally, the thought wouldn't have occurred to him, but he saw Smudge's point of view, particularly as he, Edwin, had eaten nothing all day.

"My problem is," he said, "and don't go thinking I've lost my mind or anything, but that goose…" He stopped and looked back at Blackfoot, squatting in a corner of the cart. Blackfoot scrambled up. Edwin jerked his thumb, "That particular goose, I consider too clever, to eat."

He waited for Smudge to recover from his spluttering fit and continued, "Blackfoot got us to London. When I travelled in with the farmer, he knew the way better than the horse."

Blackfoot craned his neck to the sky, which – after a long spell of cloudless blue – was now a wispy grey, and he *honked and honked, and honked.* Sparrows scattered from a nearby bush, and two baby rabbits jumped from the hedgerow. They paused, turned, and then darted back again.

"Rabbits!" yelled Smudge. "We could set traps."

"Get the goose out!"

"Yes, your Lordship!" Smudge stuck out his tongue and jumped down from the cart.

Blackfoot was ready. Smudge unhitched the tailboard, and the goose was on the ground, half flying past cart and the horse, keen to lead the way. The horse seemed happier, too, and they were soon ambling along. The pace was slow, but who cares, thought Edwin. Blackfoot kept Smudge entertained, leaving him to consider other matters.

'Other matters,' being the wheat fields, stretching as far as he could see, on either side of the road. From his high vantage point, he had a good view over the hedgerows. Why take a sudden interest in wheat, difficult to ignore, perhaps? Then he remembered the young nun telling him that farmers used soot as a fertiliser. The wheat stems with their furry tops were straight and strong, and more abundant than the wheat grown on his uncle's estate. The sun shone down, bathing the fields in rippling gold.

Edwin concentrated on the road again and marvelled at Blackfoot's stamina. The goose never seemed tired. At his own pace, he'd walk, rise and fly low for several yards then settle to a walk again. Ten miles or so later and Smudge was asleep again. Whether mesmerised by Blackfoot's antics or the slow rhythm of the cart, Edwin wasn't sure. In fact, his own shoulders slumped and his eyes… He jerked upright. No slacking, he was in charge!

After several miles, they reached a crossroads. It looked familiar. Blackfoot shot ahead, wings outstretched, head down. Sensing home? Edwin felt a flutter of anticipation himself. Where exactly was home? And more to the point, would anyone be there and how would they react? They weren't bringing welcome news.

Even the horse perked up. It lifted its head and set up a vigorous trot, almost a canter. Edwin was familiar with horses. The first time he'd ridden with hounds, he enjoyed the thrill of the chase but turned back when they reached the kill. The horse speeded up. To avoid being trampled, Blackfoot did a nifty side step. Then he spread his wings and perched on a stone obelisk at the roadside. It was a coal levy marker showing number of miles to London. Blackfoot swivelled round and ejected a smelly stream of something down the markings.

Smudge chortled.

Edwin raised his fist, "So much for wretched coal levy taxes, an abomination! So says my uncle," he yelled. Smudge gaped at him. "People out here, twenty miles from London, have to pay tax for their coal," he explained.

"So that's what them things was for!"

Edwin pulled hard on the reins. The horse was fast trotting down a narrow lane. He glanced back. Blackfoot waddled behind the cart. Things looked promising. Edwin wet his lips. Wherever they were going, it was obvious they'd soon be there.

Chapter 13
Hospitality

The country lane Edwin and Smudge were journeying down narrowed and ended. A five-barred gate faced them. The horse stopped and waited. Beyond the gate at the far end of a farmyard, Edwin noticed the thatched roof of a cottage. The roof and a jutting attic window showed above ground, indicating that the dwelling itself must be on a lower level.

Smudge jumped down from the cart. He slipped the u-shaped restraining arm off the post and pushed the gate open. The horse ambled through the gateway into the yard. Edwin could tell it was a small holding by the smell of dung, the variety of sounds and the livestock. Hens strolled around spread-toed, clucking and pecking the ground. Two cows were feeding from wire baskets attached to the outside of a barn. The baskets, Edwin discovered later, contained a mix of wheat straw, with barley, oats and beans. Cows roamed about the yard. They pulled down what they didn't eat and trampled it underfoot, where it mingled with their dung.

Smudge gave the smelly heap a professional nod of approval. "Good for fertiliser, same as what soot is," he said.

Edwin saluted Smudge. He'd opened the farmyard gate without prompting, then waited for him to pass through, and closed it again. If they were destined to be farmers then Smudge was well on the way. Edwin patted the horse's neck. The animal had done a good job, too. He glanced around for Blackfoot.

Smudge was standing at the bottom end of the yard, looking down at the cottage. Edwin approached him with the horse and cart, "Where's Blackfoot?" he called out.

"Down there."

They stood looking down at the goose as it waddled round the side of the cottage and disappeared. Almost immediately, a small girl with bright ginger curls appeared. She stopped when she saw them. With the sun behind her, the child's hair glowed round her face like a halo.

Then she opened her mouth and let out an ear-splitting yell. "Muuuu… ther!" The child moved closer, staring up at them.

She was joined by what Edwin took to be the rest of the family. Another ginger-haired child, a boy about the same age, twins, he decided, then a youngish woman and an older woman. Mother and grandmother, perhaps? They looked friendly enough as they climbed the steep steps from the cottage to greet them. The little girl ran up the steps and got there first. She clung to the horse's mane and peeped round at them.

Smudge stepped forward. "We brought 'em all back safe," he said, sweeping his arm at the horse and cart with a Smudge-like swagger.

"Good afternoon; If it is afternoon," Edwin added. "I'm afraid I've no idea what time it is." He smiled round at them all, in what he hoped was a winning manner.

There was a short pause. The older woman muttered something in response, then turned to the young woman. They frowned at each other, clearly puzzled by the farmer's absence.

Edwin opened his mouth to explain but Smudge forestalled him by gabbling on about the goose. He entertained the twins by pulling silly faces. Showing off, thought Edwin, half expecting him to stand on his hands and stick out his tongue like he did in St Albans. It worked, however, as it had with him. The twins giggled and gazed at Smudge, mesmerised by his performance.

The older woman kept looking towards the gate. When it became obvious the boys were alone, she took Edwin's arm and led him aside to ask about her husband. The younger woman joined them and introduced herself as Abigail.

Edwin tried to explain to them, that the farmer had given him a lift to London and that he'd recognised the abandoned horse and cart. "I wish I could tell you what happened to him, or where he's gone," he said. "But I don't know. We were told he'd had some sort of… blackout." He must have sounded wretched about the whole thing because the women were quick to reassure him.

The older woman smiled at him sympathetically and asked him his name.

"Ed, Eddie," he said. It slipped out quite naturally. He was getting used to his new role.

"You should be proud of yourself, Eddie. There's not many would have brought us back our horse and cart—"

"And the goose," interrupted Smudge, who had shot across the yard to join them. "Don't forget the blackfoot," he reminded them, grinning. "I never 'ad a thought 'bout them critters afore. Not apart from partaking of one of them; whenever I 'ad the chance, o' course." He wet his lips and rubbed his hands together.

Edwin shot him a look. Smudge tried to make amends. "You don't get to have no pets in the workhouse," he said. News indeed. Smudge had never said anything about his background before. But then he'd never asked him.

"No, dear," responded the older woman, and she smiled sympathetically.

"Smudge, Misses. Me name's Smudge."

"Well I'm Mrs Westcott, and Abigail is my daughter-in-law. And we're very grateful to both of you, aren't we, Abbie?"

Abigail nodded.

"What we need to explain," continued Mrs Westcott, "Is that my husband often falls asleep, particularly when he's been to market and collected supplies on the way home." She folded her arms and pursed her lips. "And he swears it's not the gin!"

Smudge looked towards the bulging sacks in the cart and asked what was in them.

"Grain and flour," she said.

"What happens when Mr Westcott falls asleep, I mean does he know when he needs to sleep, and stops off somewhere?" Edwin asked, frowning. The situation was odd and potentially dangerous; why weren't the women more concerned?

"If anyone finds him, they usually go through his pockets," Mrs Westcott replied. "My husband carries a note with the name and address of his brother's barber's shop in Camden. So that's where he'll be." The certainty in her voice, confirmed it had happened before.

"Even so," Abigail chipped in, "I do think it's time John took over; whether he wants to or not." She gave her mother-in-law a penetrating look. "We were so fortunate they were honest!"

Mrs Westcott turned to Edwin, "Do you have lodgings for the night?"

Edwin hesitated.

"We'll do yer chimbley fer free, if you let us 'ave some vittels and a stay in your barn fer the night," Smudge said, with a twin tugging on each arm.

"Please, please can they stay? Please, please…" they chanted, jumping up and down.

Abigail gave her mother-in-law a worried glance. "What about John?"

"What about him?"

"You know what he's like, and we don't take in vagrants."

"We ain't vagrants!" Smudge yelled. "We're chimbley sweeps!"

"I, I'm sorry. I didn't mean… only my husband has a bit of a temper, and—"

"He's handy with his fists," interrupted Mrs Westcott. "John's a bare-knuckle fighter. Hertfordshire champion, three years running, undefeated." She rounded on her daughter-in-law. "I'm ashamed of you, Abigail. He'll be as pleased with the boys as we are!" Abigail turned away, looking doubtful. Edwin's mouth went dry. Was there going to be trouble!

"No point waiting to find out! Come into the kitchen, lads, and I'll give you some supper."

Abigail unhitched the horse from the cart, and she and the little boy led the horse away to a nearby stable.

The little girl skipped along beside Edwin and Smudge as they followed Mrs Westcott into the cottage. "I'm Rosie," Rosie told them. And she chattered nonstop as they sat round the kitchen table.

While Mrs Westcott heated lamb stew, the boys drank mugs of milk and listened to Rosie. She doesn't need answers, Edwin thought, watching her expressive face and mouth working away.

"Is your name Smudge? You said it was. Why are you called that? 'S'pect it's cos you've got brown marks on your face, like someone's got a brush and PAINTED ALL OVER YOU. You've got one just there!" She shouted, jabbing a finger close to Smudge's left eye.

"Give over, Rosie! That's enough." Her grandmother slapped her hand away.

Rosie, undeterred, put her mouth close to Smudge's ear, and Edwin just caught her soft whisper. "We don't mind. I've got ginger hair, so's Sammy, he's got ginger hair. And we've got ginger eyebrows. So it doesn't matter you've got brown—"

"Rosie, off to bed." Abigail came in at that moment with Sammy.

The twins obediently said good night. As they left the kitchen, they pushed and shoved each other, both trying to get through the narrow doorway first.

Abigail looked after them. "They're forever at each other, those two. And it's always Rosie that wins," she said, sighing.

"We wos jus' like that," Smudge spoke out.

Edwin raised his eyebrows; this was unexpected. "Were you a twin, Smudge?"

"Close enough. Me an' me brover were born in the same year. Only he didn't live so long."

No one said anything. Smudge's face creased in a grin, "'S alright, he weren't clever like I wos!"

Abigail muttered something about seeing to the twins and left the kitchen.

Mrs Westcott left the hob and carried a pot of steaming stew to the table. She lifted the lid and a tantalising aroma of lamb and herbs and suet dumplings rose from the pot. Smudge's eyes bulged. She dipped in a ladle and stirred the contents, and Edwin could almost taste it in his mouth. Her hand poised to fill his bowl – and she stopped.

A sound outside the door.

The latch lifted.

"John—" His mother got no further.

A large man in his early thirties entered the kitchen. With a thick neck and tall enough to bend as he came through the doorway, he looked every inch a champion boxer. Straight from hedging, his sleeves were rolled high displaying tanned arms and bulging biceps. He halted on seeing Edwin and Smudge.

"What the bloody hell are—"

Huge as he was, his mother caught his arms and spun him round to face her. "Now you listen to me, John," she said, wagging a finger. "Those two lads, Eddie and…," she hesitated.

"Smudge, misses," Smudge called out.

"The lads have come all the way out from London bringing our goods in the cart. The horse is safe in the stable, and nothing is missing."

They waited.

John had his back to them.

Edwin watched him run his hands through his thick dark hair. What was he thinking? What would he do to them! Had he calmed down?

John turned. He fixed Edwin with such a fierce glare, Edwin shot to his feet ready to flee.

Mrs Westcott patted her son's arm. He didn't respond. Nevertheless, she went on to explain that his father had had 'One of his sleeping turns,' and that he'd 'been taken to his brother Silas's place in Camden.'

"You can't know that for sure!" John barked out the words without turning, his eyes still boring into Edwin.

Edwin curled up his toes.

Smudge suddenly stepped forward, hand extended. "Pleased to make yer acquaintance… Mr John…" His hand hovered in the space between them.

John transferred his glare to Smudge. "Well?" He barked again at his mother.

Mrs Westcott shrugged. She came back to the table, her gesture conveying, 'I'm not answering if you shout.' Edwin clenched his fists and spoke for her.

"I'm afraid we're not sure of your father's exact whereabouts, sir. We were only told that he had been taken."

John's eyes narrowed. He stepped closer to him. "You sound honest enough." He jerked his head in Smudge's direction. "Where did you pick up the young Cockney?"

"London, sir. Master sweep Mrs Bridger, Swallow Street." Edwin hoped he'd said enough to satisfy him.

"That one of your sacks in the cart?" Edwin glanced at Smudge. "Don't look like there's soot in it!" John swung round, glaring down at Smudge for an answer.

Smudge scowled, "I ain't stolen nofink, if that's what you wos finking!"

"Darned right!" His big chin jutted forward.

Mrs Westcott stepped between them. "Give over, John. The lad's good with the twins, and he's done us a favour."

The big man pressed his lips together and frowned. "Eat your supper up. You can stay the night in the barn." So saying, John swung away and went back outside.

Mrs Westcott watched him go. She then ladled the lamb stew into their bowls with a crooked smile on her face. "You'll be all right with him, so long as he keeps off the drink," she said.

Chapter 14
At the Farm

Early the following morning, Edwin emerged from the hay barn into an empty yard. A grey mist hung low in the sky but the air was warm, with a hint of mugginess. They could be in for a storm. Edwin stood for a few minutes with his eyes closed. Falling asleep so quickly the night before, he'd not had time to think about things and file them in his mind. No point letting a new experience slip away, like the frog he'd once caught.

His memory was good; he'd had enough practice at school. Equations and tables, poetry and text, all written and learned by rote. This was different. Everything was new. Write it all down. He told himself. Record everything he'd experienced, good and bad. Soon as he could. The excitement of yesterday's events, together with the best food he'd tasted since… certainly not the meagre school meals that pupils ate with their teachers.

'Conducive to learning,' Father Cornelius told them. Or worse, meals at Richmorton Hall, where the table overflowed with a shocking abundance of food. Aunt Elizabeth however, pecked at her food like a sparrow.

'I'll just try a little of every dish,' was her mealtime tweet. She did so, mainly to please kitchen staff who'd be unemployed with nothing to cook. And there was always enough spare to take home for their families. As for him, his aunt had her suspicions about Abbey School food and urged him to eat heartily, which on reflection, was just as well.

So, after a good meal and restful night on a bed of hay with a horse blanket, how did he feel? Good. He was pleased with himself. Yesterday, he'd taken charge and made decisions.

A hard shove in the small of his back, and he pitched forward and fell to his knees. He opened his eyes and for a ghastly moment thought it was Scurvy Sam!

"What you standin' about moonin' for?" It was Smudge.

He could have bashed him. Pushed him to the ground, sat on him and plastered his stupid grinning face with DUNG! And he would have, he would have... But, Blackfoot chose that moment to come flying around the corner of the farmhouse; neck down, wings outstretched. On seeing them, the goose adopted a more normal posture. Just as though, Edwin thought, calming down, afraid they might leave without saying goodbye. Or maybe Blackfoot had come to warn them of something.

The goose approached him making gobbling noises in his throat. Then he circled around Smudge and hissed. Smudge lunged for Blackfoot's neck. And missed. Edwin laughed as Smudge backed away scowling.

Nevertheless, Smudge did go with him as they followed Blackfoot round to the back of the farmhouse cottage.

They weren't the only ones up, he discovered. Cows munched grass in a nearby field. Hens pecked the ground all round them, and Mrs Westcott and Abigail sat on low stools plaiting long-stemmed straw. He watched Abigail draw a straw through her teeth, shredding it down its length, and caught a glimpse of her lower teeth. They were blackened by the constant action. No wonder she never smiled.

A door was open behind them. It revealed a narrow hall, where Edwin could see straw bonnets hanging from pegs in the wall. The product, he guessed of weeks of labour. Were they orders from customers? He wondered. His Aunt Elizabeth had her straw bonnets delivered by hand.

Mrs Westcott saw him looking at the bonnets. "We've been decorating them for a lady in high society," she told him proudly. "Abigail is good with her ribbons and bows." Abigail went a shade of pink, but seemed pleased.

Edwin tensed his shoulders. They ought to get going. He glanced round for Smudge. Judging from giggles nearby, Smudge was distracting the twins from their work, demonstrating how to climb 'treacle' chimneys.

"Treacle chimbleys! Chimbleys! Chimbleys!" chanted the twins, delighted by his cockney pronunciation. They sat beside him and there were more joyful shrieks when he curled up on the ground, pretending to be stuck in a 'foggy hole.'

Abigail interrupted them. "Rosie," she called out, "Get to your measuring."

The little girl got to her feet. It was obvious now that her twin brother was the slower of the two and less intelligent. Edwin watched her gather up a long coil of plaited straw. Her brother held the end of the coil while she measured it.

Edwin asked what she was doing.

"Measuring scores. I learned it at plait school," she piped up. "One score's twenty yards."

"Twenty yards," repeated her brother, brandishing a yard measure made of wood round his head.

Edwin addressed the little boy. "How do you plait the straw, Sammy?" Sammy looked up eager to show what he could do. He picked up one end of the plait and clumsily twisted a strand of straw—

"Not like that, stupid!" Rose snatched the plait from her brother. Sammy desperately tried to get it back; biting his lower lip and trembling. Rosy slapped his hand away.

"Give it back!" Edwin spoke coldly to the little girl. He brought his face close, eyeballing her. He was being deliberately menacing, remembering how frightened and defenceless it felt being bullied.

"I'm sure you didn't mean to be a bully," he said quietly. Rosy sucked in her breath and looked miserable. She'd understood.

"I'll help you, Sammy," she said, switching to an engaging smile. And she guided her brother's hand round the straw. "Then you can show the young gentleman."

He remained long enough for Sammy to prove he could plait (almost) as well as his sister, and then moved away. Rosy was still happily encouraging her brother when he looked back. Edwin felt ten feet tall. He thrust out his chest and allowed himself a moment of pride.

"There's a bundle of bread and cheese for you both," said Mrs Westcott. "It's in the kitchen. And John said to tell you, he'd be waiting in the cart, down the lane."

Smudge had joined them and overheard. What's he want us to do?"

"John doesn't want anything done." Mrs Westcott chuckled, "He wants to take you to the Horse Fair, as a reward."

Smudge looked mystified. "Reward, what's that then?"

Edwin was about to explain, when Mrs Westcott turned to him and said:

"John will be boxing, if you've a mind to watch." And she added, "If you can keep him from drinking, I'd be grateful."

Edwin nodded and smiled, but felt uneasy. He wished he was heading back to London. On the other hand, it was sad that Smudge had never had a reward.

Chapter 15
Break Up

The mist had drifted, but no sun shone on the threesome in the cart. Edwin sat in the back with Smudge, while John took the horse for a speedy jog down the country lanes.

Throwing an occasional remark over his shoulder, John revealed that he hadn't boxed for some time, but he needed a win that day for a particular reason.

Smudge prodded his arm, "What's he saying, Ed?"

Edwin leaned forward and attracted John's attention. "May we know the reason, sir?"

John laughed. "I doubt you'd understand if I told you," he said.

"You wish to retain the championship?"

"Ay, there's that. But I need the purse that comes with it to buy a sheen for the wife."

Edwin guessed a 'purse' was money for a win, but he'd never heard of a sheen. He sat back and folded his arms, wishing himself elsewhere. He was keeping a look out, but was probably being paranoid; his family never attended country fairs, so it was unlikely he'd be seen.

When they arrived at the fairground field, they had to wait. Ahead of them the double gates leading into the field stood open and inviting. With no entrance fee, a constant stream of country folk dressed in their Sunday best, jostled to enter. There were horse-drawn carts of various sizes competing for room with large numbers of donkeys strung together. Braying with excitement, the donkeys forced foot passengers to let them through.

Edwin cheered up, amused to see their jockeys dressed in an assortment of colours walking behind them.

Their appearance caused Smudge to leap from the cart and pump the hand of a young man he'd recognised. A merry exchange took place. Then Smudge climbed back in the cart again.

"One of me chummies, come to ride in the Derby." He grinned and pointed. "Donkey Derby, Ed. Them's mostly sweeps."

A chummy. Edwin looked away, wondering if he'd ever become one.

They waited until the crowd thinned. When only a few stragglers remained, instead of driving forward, John dismounted. Leaving the horse to nibble the short grass, he asked them to 'join him in a prayer.' Smudge's eyes bulged. Edwin grinned and gave him a dig in the ribs. John knelt at the side of the cart and pulled a leather-bound bible from his pocket.

Smudge pressed close, following John's moving finger across the text, and it occurred to Edwin that the climbing boy could neither read nor write. That gave him an idea, perhaps he could teach him. John's eyes closed and his lips moved in silent prayer. Was he asking God to help him win his fight?

John got to his feet, took the horse's reins and led the cart into the fairground. Without mentioning a word about what had happened, Edwin and Smudge followed.

After tethering the horse to a stake with several others, John left them.

Edwin found it impossible not to enjoy the atmosphere of the fair. And he was certainly seeing life! With no money to spend, he and Smudge watched while burly men knocked coconuts off shies, and gawped at women with enormous bosoms. The women stood on a platform outside a tent enticing clients to step inside and 'savour their delights', whatever they were.

The beer tent, with its raucous laughter and smell of local brewed cider was already full inside, and overflowed outside with countrymen holding tankards of ale. Edwin hoped John wasn't one of them, and he remembered Mrs Westcott's bundle of bread and cheese. He sat on the grass with Smudge and divided the food between them. They chewed slowly.

"Best make it last, 's long as you can," Smudge instructed him. Good sense when regular meals were a thing of the past.

On the far side of the field Edwin spotted what appeared to be the top of a large tent. A circus had taken root! The attraction proved too much. They crammed the last of the bread in their mouths and raced across the field.

Edwin followed Smudge round to the back of the main marquee. Smudge seemed to know what he was doing, and he told him to lie down close to the tent pole and pretend to be asleep.

"The dodge," he whispered, lying next to him, "is to wait fer a bit, then t' roll quick under the tent flap." He'd chosen the exact spot inside, behind the raised seats, he said. "So's they could climb up and sit like Lords at the top, and none the wiser."

All went according to plan, except for a small dog. The mongrel wrinkled its nose at the smell of them and it snapped at their heels and yelped. Fortunately, the roar of caged lions and the crack of the ringmaster's whip drowned the dog's pathetic barks.

Inside the arena, a wall of scaffolding faced them. It supported tiers of bench-type seats that rose to the top of the tent. Unseen, Edwin and Smudge climbed up the backs of the seating and swung themselves over the top bench. As Smudge had predicted, they were high enough to look down, and lord it over all who sat below.

Edwin hugged himself; it was a big plus – being able to climb. He slapped Smudge on the shoulder and declared him a, "jolly good fellow."

Smudge beamed.

They sat side by side and watched waltzing ponies and a performing poodle in a frilly skirt. Then four Alsations ran into the arena. The dogs promptly sat on their haunches, waiting. Trainers followed them, carrying hoops on frames and smouldering torches. They set the hoops alight.

The audience cheered and cheered.

Edwin froze and gripped his trembling knees. Smudge leapt up. The climbing boy yelled with excitement as the hoops spun on their frames, ablaze with smoke and tongues of fire. At the sound of a whistle the dogs raced round the circle of hoops, then each dog turned and leapt through a flaming hoop. Then turned and leapt again.

Deafened by cheers Edwin whispered his thoughts out loud. "The dogs are trained, trained," he repeated to himself. "They are trained to have no fear." And his heartbeat slowed, and the blood flowed back through his veins. He could do that.

He wiped the sweat from his forehead. And he watched the dogs, and he smiled, admiring their courage. Then he clapped with the audience when the flames died down and the dogs were rewarded. They leapt about. The dogs were happy. So was he. He had conquered his fear.

Everyone waited while the arena cleared.

There was a deafening roll of drums, and the ringmaster entered with a clown to entertain them.

Smudge leaned forward and gave him a grin.

The clown swivelled round on his heels, bowing and smiling at his audience. He looked up and shouted out, "Master, I fear we are going to have a storm."

"Indeed," the ringmaster replied. "How can that be, for the weather outside appears fine. I think you have made a mistake."

"Well," said the clown, and he pointed straight up at Smudge. "Look up there, there's a black cloud whether or no."

All eyes turned towards them.

While Smudge good-humouredly joined in the laughter, Edwin shrank within himself. He turned away, and it looked like he'd distanced himself from Smudge.

The laughter died, and the clown moved on to another unsuspecting victim. Edwin, catching Smudge's painful glare, moved to reach out to him, to explain….

But Smudge left his side and slid from sight down the scaffolding and out through the marquee the way they had entered.

Edwin followed, desperately wanting to tell him he'd feared the sudden public attention. That someone may have been in the audience who knew his family, or heard of his disappearance. And that he didn't want to be found. It wasn't anything to do with Smudge or his way of life. He wanted to be with him, to be his chummy. Edwin wiped away a tear and rolled out from under the tent.

A large sandalled foot trod hard on his hand. He couldn't get up! The sandal smelt of the sea, the leather cracked and whitened by salt. Edwin raised his chin. His eye travelled up the sailor's trouser leg, and he recognised the wide leather belt. He knew who it was.

Scurvy Sam!

He gulped down a lump in his throat. Now he was done for!

"I've trapped yer good and proper. Should have recognised you first time, you being so puny still."

Edwin rebelled at the sneer and wriggled his hand free. Sam yanked him upright, clasping him tight to his belt. He only reached the sailor's waist. He winced as the metal buckle scraped his cheek, and he could hardly breathe.

"Eh! Eh!" A coarse chuckle from Sam lips and a whiff of foul ale. "That banker will have t' believe me now. Now I've got you, I'll get the reward," he snarled.

Sam had his arms pinned but his legs were free. If he had shoes on he'd kick him; kick him in the shins. He had to do something. He thought wildly. Come on, Edwin, come on!

He opened his mouth and screamed and screamed! He even frightened himself. Had his voice broken?

People turned and stared. Above the noise of the fair-ground he'd made himself heard. But Sam was no fool. He swung Edwin round to face them.

"Caught him thieving! And not for the first time, neither. But he'll not escape me now!" Sam told them.

And they moved away.

All but one.

Edwin's heart thumped even louder. Friend or Foe?

A voice called out: "Been on the look-out for you." John came up to them. "Fight was over quicker 'n I thought." The boxer's face was flushed. He had a swelling over one eye, and his speech was slurred.

Sam slackened his hold.

Whether he knew the bare-knuckle fighter or not, the two were well matched. John seemed not to notice his captor and spoke directly to him. "Look, lad, look what I got for her; the love of my life, my Abigail." He thrust something into Edwin's hands – a wooden box, stained with blood from his knuckles. "It's a sheen, 's what we call it. To press straw flat for plaiting,"

A movement from Sam.

Then it was over.

With a crunch, John's fist smashed into Sam's nose. He followed it with a left hook and an uppercut to Sam's chin. Scurvy Sam went down with a moan. They were attracting attention. Edwin darted forward, desperate to get away.

John's hand shot out and grabbed his shirtfront. He snatched the sheen from his hand as though afraid he might run off with it. In fact, John's whole manner changed.

"Better hop it quick." He spat the words in Edwin's face: "I'm tempted by the reward that's out for you."

Edwin gasped.

John released him and stepped back. Before turning away, he thrust several coins in his hand, muttering, "You did us a favour."

Edwin pocketed the coins. Then he thought about Smudge. Where did he go? He had to find him! The show being over, people were streaming out of the marquee. In his haste, Edwin stumbled over a tent rope. He over-balanced, righted himself, and then set off again. Not knowing where to look for Smudge he glanced about as he ran. Bypassing a chestnut seller with customers queuing, he'd a ghastly feeling in the pit of his stomach he'd seen Scurvy Sam! No, impossible, he'd left him unconscious.

To be safe, Edwin raced away from the tents and headed for a stretch of open field. He stopped midway, unable to run further. His breath came out in gulps. He looked back. Nobody following. Edwin put a hand to his eyes and stared into the distance, trying to focus. He noticed a small copse bordering the field, then a movement by the trees!

Was it Smudge?

The sky darkened. A plop of rain dribbled down his nose. Others followed. It splattered down, then came fast, drumming the hardened ground. Intent on finding Smudge, he'd not noticed the change of weather and he was out in the open getting soaked. There was a rumble of thunder overhead, and a zip of lightning streaked the sky. Edwin stumbled across the field, his feet squelching in the long grass. The ground, too hard to absorb the sudden deluge, became a bog. Rain plastered hair to his face and his nostrils burned with the smell of thirsty earth.

"Blimey. You look a sight!"

He'd reached the edge of the copse. No explanation. No malice, no ill feelings. Just Smudge, standing under a Beech tree, grinning. Edwin could have hugged him. Despite sheltering with his sack across his shoulders, Smudge was as wet as he was. They stood under the tree, while rainwater poured through the branches, forming a lake at their feet.

More flashes of light. An ear-splitting CRACK!

And lightning struck a nearby tree. It split straight down the trunk. A section broke away and fell towards them. He was off. Edwin tore away from the copse heading further across the open field. No idea where. Just get away. Find shelter. Difficult to see through blinding rain – His foot struck a stone, and he pitched forward, falling spread-eagled to his face. He got to his feet spitting grass from his mouth.

Smudge had caught up with him. His face, washed clean by rain was scowling. "Where you goin'?"

"Anywhere away from here!"

"What's spookin' you out, Ed?"

There was no way he was mentioning Scurvy Sam. "I met up with John," he said. "And there's a reward out for me!" Smudge's face switched to a broad grin. "I can't stay here. I'm going back to London," he shouted.

Smudge was still grinning! He shoved him hard in the shoulder. He didn't move, he couldn't. Nor could he. They'd sunk to their ankles in mud. Edwin glared at Smudge. Had he not heard him? He cupped his hands against the rain half-drowning them, and shouted, "I said, that there's a reward—"

"I—heard—yer! 'An what's to stop me gettin' the reward meself!" Smudge yelled back.

For a moment, he couldn't breathe. The possibility never occurred to him. "You don't even know what it is! What would you do with it?" He sneered.

"Give it t' me chummy, Jake. He'd know what t' do wiv it oright."

"I thought I was your chummy!"

"Not yet you ain't."

The row was decided by a thunder roll and a flash of light in the sky. It lit up the edge of the field. Edwin's heartbeat quickened. He saw the mast of a vessel. It was swinging backwards and forwards in the gale, in what could be – must be, a river!

He plucked his feet from the mud. Not caring if Smudge followed him or not, he slogged his way across the field towards it. Sure enough, tied to a tall post in the river was a smart-looking barge. Its single sail was down, and the mast dipped and swayed at the side of the bank. Edwin waited for the right moment and then leapt aboard. Still in a crouched position he glanced around. A tarpaulin – left on deck.

He dived underneath.

The canvass tarpaulin covered a heap of coal dust and some sacking. His teeth chattered, and he hugged his knees. This would do, nicely, he decided. Quite like home – his new home in Swallow Street. Edwin burrowed into the sacking and curled up. As the small craft lurched from side to side, he had doubts about the mooring. Listening to the rain strumming the tarpaulin and battering the surrounding deck, worrying thoughts flashed through his mind. He was a stowaway… in a rocking ship. The rope may snap at any moment… carry him away… down river… out to sea… to drown, drown….

Chapter 16
Rumours

In the Wilde's Islington residence, the family were sitting down to a meal. More family members present than usual. Mary smiled at her mother, Charlotte, sitting in her chair at the end of the table. More often than not, her mother's chair was vacant at meal times.

Charlotte Wilde was conversing with her father's two older sisters. Both were spinsters and known as the Miss Peas because of their likeness to each other. They'd arrived from Brighton for a brief stay. Two years apart in age, their cheeks glowed with health from the sea breezes. And they thrived on gossip.

"Elizabeth will be joining us shortly," her father told them. The sisters arched their eyebrows at each other.

Mary sucked in her breath. She *did* like her aunts; they amused her, *normally*. There was nothing *normal*, however, about Edwin's continued disappearance! She pressed her lips together, annoyed. To make matters worse, her mother joined in the conversation.

"I was so embarrassed when Sister Ignatius called to see me," Charlotte said. "The Nunnery sisters are very kind to me, you know. Their herbal remedies have done me no end of good." She paused. "They seemed to think that Edwin had stolen one of their platters! We are all upset, and so embarrassed," she repeated and stopped. Her words hung in the air.

Mary let go her frustrations, "I don't understand why you can't all *see* that Edwin has been done an *injustice!*"

"Mary!" Her father rose from his chair.

"Edwin is no thief. Why should he be? What's a platter to him! Anyway, I've seen him," Mary yelled. "And he wasn't alone; he was with three chimney sweep boys. And they seemed to be friends!"

She fled from the room, leaving the family gaping after her.

Further north, in Hertfordshire, a smart barge sailed downriver with Daniel Porter at the helm. Navigation was unhurried, due to storm debris. A large branch of driftwood, remnants of a torn sail, and a section of broken crate bobbed alongside in the water.

In the stern of the boat, a corner of the tarpaulin lifted. Water streamed to the deck as Edwin crawled out. He must have fallen asleep. For how long, he'd no idea. He stood upright and stretched his arms. Glimpsing back, it appeared they'd travelled quite a way, and he was at the mercy of the skipper. He saw him now, standing at the wheel, looking straight ahead. A tall man, not dressed as a sailor, by the cut of his clothes, more like a merchant, Edwin decided.

"Here goes." He thrust his shoulders back, and walked stiff-legged with cramp, towards his unknown captor.

Daniel turned. "So, you've woken."

Edwin stepped back. The skipper knew he was on board!

"Checked the tarpaulin soon as I boarded," Daniel informed him as though reading his thoughts.

Edwin shot out a hand to steady himself against the roll of the barge. The action helped calm his nerves as they studied each other. The skipper eyed him up and down taking his time, his brow furrowed as though something registered that he may be more than an urchin stowaway. To a discerning gentleman the cut of his breeches and shirt, although dirty and torn, had probably betrayed him. No matter, the man's eyes were friendly and he spoke like a London tradesman.

"I apologise for boarding your vessel, sir," Edwin said, after a longish pause. "And hope I may travel with you to London."

The Skipper regarded him quizzically. "Have you a mind to be a sailor?"

"No, sir. But I have some knowledge of the sea."

111

Daniel squinted at him, "Do you indeed?" He sounded amused. "Then take the wheel while I go below."

Edwin took the wheel from his grasp. The well-crafted wheel felt smooth to his hands, and he revised his first impression. Despite evidence of a recent cargo of coal, this wasn't a rough-hewn river-trader's barge. And it had been entrusted to *him*. He thrust out his chest and glanced up at the sail. It billowed in a forward breeze, its former redness a faded pink.

The skipper came up the steps from the cabin holding two tankards of ale. Edwin nodded his thanks and took one from him. He kept his eyes fixed on the river as he put the tankard to his lips and drank. It was strong ale, something he wasn't accustomed to, but grateful for something to drink, he willed himself not to cough and splutter. The skipper downed his ale in one gulp.

"Well," he said, watching him for a while. "I see you're no milk and water seaman; a master mariner, or a pirate maybe. Is that more in your line?"

"My father taught me to sail."

"Oh and where might that have been?"

"Constantinople."

"Turkey, eh! So, what's his son doing as a stowaway?"

Edwin gulped. What should he say?

The skipper pushed him aside and seized the wheel. "We're nearing the New River head. The current can be dangerous," he said.

Edwin watched him bring the wheel under control, then ventured to ask, "May I know your name, sir?"

"Daniel Porter, late of Camden, now of Marylebone. And you?" Edwin hesitated. Daniel intervened, "You give yourself away by—"

"My name is Eddie Hall," he lied. "I'm a scholar, absconded from boarding school. Have no further use for Latin and Greek. I mostly know the language and I wish to seek my fortune elsewhere."

"Aye, I thought as much. And I suspect, my young sir, you are not who you appear to be."

"Nor you, sir."

112

Daniel slapped his thighs and chortled. He then told Edwin to go below and change his clothes. "My boys are about your size," he said.

"You have sons, sir?"

"No, I have daughters. At present, two are doing the Grand Tour abroad with my wife. They will return, no doubt, with artefacts and frippery, when some knowledge of classical architecture would be more useful," he paused. His voice softened with affection. "My youngest, Sophia, is home nursing one of my boys. The lad has a fever."

Edwin remained silent, baffled by what he'd heard. So, who were the *boys!* No doubt he'd find out. As instructed, he left Daniel and went below.

Inside the cabin, a large table took up much of the space. Edwin stared in surprise; his attention caught by what was on the table. Plans and drawings covered most of the surface. He moved close and gazed down at them. There were sketches of fireplaces and chimneys and the interior rooms of large houses, all drawn in astonishing detail. If only he had time, he'd happily study them for hours! The rest of the table held a large amount of stationary; quill pens, bottles of ink and a pile of cut parchment. A tingle ran down his spine and he gripped the edge of the table. First things first, he told himself.

He found a trunk full of clothes and pulled out a pair of breeches, two shirts and a waistcoat. Edwin stripped off. The clothes weren't new but clean. They felt good. He'd almost forgotten the feel of clean clothes. His own garments were damp and smelly. But they did belong to him, his only possessions. And, he admitted, giving them a last look before bundling them up, his only connection with the past. He'd need a sack to put them in!

Edwin returned to the deck keeping a wary eye on Daniel. Camden Lock was coming into view. They must be further down river than he'd supposed. Daniel's gaze remained focused dead ahead. Edwin grabbed a sack from under the tarpaulin and shot back to the cabin.

This time, he was after the stationary. And he'd better get a move on. An idea had come to him. Daniel was obviously a wealthy architect. If he took, or rather, borrowed a few items, surely Daniel wouldn't notice the loss. Whereas, he, Edwin, needed them. He'd neither money nor means of purchase. Travelling stationers, trading in St Paul's churchyard, would sneer at the few coins he possessed.

Edwin selected a quill, a small bottle of ink, and counted out six sheets of parchment. He pondered for a moment and then decided to leave a note. Dipping the quill in the ink, he wrote:

'*My esteemed friend, I am in need of writing material. I will repay you in full at some later date. In gratitude. Eddie Hall.*'

He signed his name with a flourish. Then he rolled up the paper he'd commandeered, added the quill, and secured the two together with string. He stowed the ink in his bundled up clothes and stuffed everything in the sack. The coins John had given him he placed together with his note on a plan Daniel was working on and turned to leave. Something made him halt. He stared at the plan. It showed a sketch of an unfinished terrace of mansions. And one large mansion on its own. A scribbled heading at the top of the plan read, No 1 Richmorton House. His uncle and aunt's new mansion!

He quickly recovered. Nothing to worry about. Daniel didn't know who he was. And what did it matter; he'd soon be lost again in London City. Edwin returned to the deck, dumped his sack near the ship's boarding side ready for departure, and joined Daniel.

Daniel saluted him when he offered his help. With a strong wind blowing and little natural light, lowering and securing the sail, would have proved difficult for a lone sailor. They said little, but a friendship had sprung up between them, an empathy; each aware what the other was thinking, yet not voicing their thoughts. Edwin suspected that Daniel had sent him down to his cabin, knowing he'd discover the connection with his uncle and aunt. If this was true why did Daniel remain silent about his identity? They both had secrets.

When they reached Camden, his parting with Daniel was brief. Daniel seemed eager to get home to his daughter. Before he left, however, he handed Edwin a folded sheet of paper, then clapped him on the shoulder with a warning:

"Look out for yourself, son. Rioters have burned Newgate jail and criminals let free."

Edwin thanked him and they parted. He couldn't wait to read Daniel's paper and searched for the nearest gas lamp. As soon as he unfolded it, he knew what it was.

A trade card.

Even so, he gasped with shock. Daniel Porter, a Master Sweep!

He'd never seen such an impressive card! Scrolled and headed by the Royal Coat of Arms, it advertised the patronage of HRH Princess Amelia, King George III's daughter. Etched columns down either side revealed membership of the Order of Masons. Written across the centre of the card the master sweep claimed to *'rectify and make operable, smoakey chimnies and coppers, thought incurable by 'Eminent professors'*, adding: *'no cure no pay.'*

At the bottom of the card was an illustrated scene. Edwin peered at it for some time. It depicted an area in a wealthy part of London where Daniel stood outside a Government building with a well-dressed client and four apprentices. Edwin smiled to himself. The boys' clothes looked familiar. The apprentice sweeps had sacks over their shoulders, and they carried short-handled brushes and scrapers.

The card also advertised Daniel as a Soot Trader. That, and much else besides, thought Edwin. Daniel was an architect. Edwin laughed and bounced on his toes, delighted that a chimney sweep could rise to such success. It made him stop and think. He'd head for St Paul's and start writing.

He took some time to get there. Heeding Daniel's warning about released criminals from Newgate he avoided the main thoroughfare. One person was already out to get him! And there may be more. His skin went clammy at the thought. He jumped at shadows looming in doorways, and the evening traffic seemed to get louder as he hurried up Ludgate hill.

As he'd hoped, when sinking down on the topmost step, the great cathedral with its gas lamps and well-lit steps made a good place for writing. Edwin opened his sack and removed his writing materials. He was eager to start. But the words wouldn't

115

come; his thoughts and emotions a jumbled mess. Too tired? Too late in the day?

A plan. He needed a plan.

A place to start.

A TITLE!

Edwin transferred his gaze from the late evening carriages labouring up Ludgate Hill towards the cathedral, and he wrote:

EDWIN'S JOURNEY, *in Pursuit of Being a Chummy*. It had a good ring to it. Edwin hesitated. Now wasn't the time to do it. It could wait. He put everything back in his sack and stood up. He'd go back to Swallow Street, see if Smudge was there.

Chapter 17
Number Three Swallow Street

"Joe, it's Ed come back to us."

The little boy's happy cry cheered Edwin as he slid down the coal-chute into Bess Carter's cellar. It was risky, coming back not knowing if he'd be welcome. The trapdoor banged behind him. He picked himself up and dusted the coal from his clean clothes. The light from a flickering candle showed the faces of Joe and Pete. Both were smiling, looking pleased to see him. He peered round the rest of cellar. No sign of Smudge or Jake. He moved towards the brothers.

"Where's Smudge?" He directed his question at Joe.

Pete scrambled to his feet, pulling him down beside them. "You are pleased to see us, aren't you, Ed?"

"Of course I am, Pete, just worried about Smudge. We got caught in a storm, and I don't know what happened to him."

"Smudge was lucky Jake let him have a few days off. He wouldn't have done if he hadn't been distracted." Joe sounded peeved.

"What's distracted, Joe?"

"Not got his mind on the job." He turned to Edwin, "So where've you been?"

"Hertfordshire. We went to a circus, Pete." The little boy's eyes sparkled in the candlelight.

"Could we do that, Joe? 'Stead of going to see the Wild Boy?" He tugged at Edwin's arm, "Joe's been telling me 'bout the Wild Boy. He's called Peter like me. Don't want to see him. I want to go to—"

"What wild boy?" Edwin asked, wanting to draw the conversation away from circuses, wishing he'd never mentioned it. It made him shudder, thinking about what might have happened if John hadn't saved him. It was best put behind him.

"Shall I tell you about Peter, the wild boy?" Joe's voice cut through his thoughts.

"Was he the one found in Hanover, in Hertswood Forest, living wild like an animal?" Edwin said.

"You know a lot."

Was Joe impressed? Or annoyed? He couldn't fathom him out; the boy's tone of voice gave nothing away and his face was in shadows. He felt uncomfortable though; had he been showing off when he'd rather make friends? Edwin addressed both of them and tried again.

"I'm not too familiar with London, Joe. I bet you know lots of interesting places to take Pete."

The little boy nodded excitedly. "Oooo yes," he squealed. "Joe took me danci…" The rest of his words were lost.

Edwin was sure Pete was about to say *dancing,* but a sudden flame from the candle caught the movement of Joe's outstretched arm and alarmed face; as though warning Pete to keep quiet.

"I took you to watch *fencing,* didn't I, Pete? He sometimes gets confused," Joe explained, turning to him.

"Yes, yes and they had on these funny clothes." Pete giggled. His giggles turned into laughter. Edwin put a finger to his lips and pointed up, concerned their mistress might hear.

"We needn't worry," Joe told him. "Mistress is ill again and can't move. Confined to bed, so we've been told."

"It's been good for us, Ed. Me and Joe took food from the kitchen."

Edwin smiled, thinking Pete looked the better for it. "What's wrong with her?" he asked.

"Dropsy. She drinks too much gin." Joe reached under some sacking and removed a covered dish. "We can get more." He handed Edwin a wedge of something to eat.

"Thanks." Edwin stuffed the food in his mouth. It was tasteless, whatever it was, but welcome. The brothers regarded him in silence while he ate. When he'd finished, he asked again about Jake.

Joe shrugged. "As I said, we've not seen much of him. He gives directions where to go, and I and Pete do what's needed. Not much chimney sweeping now it's warmer. Mostly, we core new flues of rubble."

"I don't like bringing down bird's nests, Joe. Not with little eggs in."

"No, me neither."

Edwin persisted, "Where does Jake go; what does he do?" Joe remained silent. Edwin turned to Pete. Pete opened his mouth and shut it again at Joe's look. He leaned close, however, and whispered, "Not s'posed to say, but he goes off with Mr Wills."

Edwin changed the subject. If it was a secret he didn't want to get Pete into trouble and asked instead about the wild boy.

"He was brought to England…" Joe's voice continued in darkness as the candle flickered and died.

Edwin only half listened. He couldn't warm to Joe, like he did to little Pete. Yet they were about the same age, Joe slightly taller. They should be friends. The boy struck him as being educated. Was that it? Joe made him feel less superior!

"… They couldn't teach him to talk. He's still alive. People pay to visit him," Joe was saying.

Edwin tried to push his negative thoughts aside and show an interest. "He must be quite old. I wonder what he looks like."

"I can tell you." *Here we go!* Edwin inwardly groaned. "I've seen a portrait of him, of when he was younger." Joe fully described him. Pete's eyelids were drooping.

"He won't look like that now!" Edwin found himself retorting.

"Of course, he won't! He's 68! His complexion is healthy, and he has a full white beard. He can say 'Peter' and 'King George' and hum a bit. And he understands what you say to him!"

So there! That told him! Edwin's nostrils flared.

Pete perked up. "Smudge will be back soon, Ed. He's got to sweep King George Tavern, tomorrow." He wrinkled his nose at Jo as if to say, I remembered, you didn't.

Edwin thanked him.

The little boy lay down and closed his eyes, a happy smile on his face.

"The King George is over in the Shoreditch area." Jo said, as he moved away. "I don't think Smudge will be here tonight. I'll give you directions if you like."

Edwin shook out his sleeping sack. "I know where it is," he called back. He didn't, but he'd find out.

"Good night, then."

Like a voice from the past. His mother had always wished him good night. Unexpected tears pricked behind his eyes.

"'Night," he called back.

He was still awake several hours later. The occasional loud voice and rumble of night-time carriages from the street above had dwindled. He was comfortable enough in his corner and warm in his clean clothes, but sleep wouldn't come. His damp clothes! Remembering them, he got up and shook out his sack. As he laid his clothes on the coal heap to dry he had an idea. Might be dangerous, but worth trying.

Edwin picked up his writing materials and made his way round the coal heap. He tiptoed past the sleeping forms of Joe and Pete, towards the cellar door. He smelt the cold dampness of the wall before he touched it. It was darker this side of the cellar and he had to feel along the wall for the doorframe. Further to the left. Success! The door latch.

His forehead prickled with alarm. A sudden vision of Bess came to mind. What if she was behind the door, her huge body blocking the stairs! He'd stab her with his quill! She was so fat though, she'd never notice. He sucked in his breath and pressed down on the latch. He left the door ajar and climbed the steps. Gaslight filtered down from a semi-circle of glass in the front door. Edwin moved to the staircase. His shoulder blades tightened. Dreading what he may see, his eyes travelled upwards to the landing. No sound from above.

Edwin crept down the narrow hall to the kitchen. He'd remembered the smell of cabbage when he'd left the house before with Jake and Smudge. He chuckled to himself. Good fortune favoured the brave. He'd no way of knowing from the cellar, but the skies had cleared and a full moon shone through the window at the back of the house. It illuminated the kitchen which was small and bare. Had Joe tidied up, so as not to leave evidence of taking food from Bess's larder?

There was plenty of light. Edwin pulled a bench to the table and sat down. He unrolled his paper. Five sheets. He considered them for a moment. Then he flattened a sheet, dipped his pen in the ink and drew a line across half way, dividing the paper into two halves. Two days either side on each page, five pages, twenty days. Enough for now, he decided.

Not sure of the date or day of the week he stared up at the moon. It was maddening not knowing! He thought back. School had broken up on Friday...? He'd begin with today, easiest to remember. Edwin wrote *MAY 1780, TODAY*. To keep focused, he penned, *YESTERDAY*, below the halfway line and planned to work backwards and put dates in later. Three or four sentences should do for each day, and any conversation recorded in Latin. For privacy. He grinned at the thought and began writing.

It must have been several hours later. Edwin realised he'd fallen asleep when his head drooped forward and a blob of ink fell on his paper. The moon had almost disappeared. Flowing script covered three and a half sides of his paper. He'd managed seven days, working backwards, heading each section, *THE DAY BEFORE*, and reached Friday, the day he'd met the boys. One thing more. He inserted a small diagram of flues in the margin. Satisfied, he gathered up his writing materials and returned to the cellar.

As Edwin settled again in his sleeping sack, he reminded himself that Smudge would be sweeping the King George Tavern in the morning. He'd get up early and go and help him, he decided. That's if he could find the tavern! His eyes closed.

Chapter 18
Capture

The gypsy girl wore a large earring and a light shawl round her shoulders. She fluttered her eyelashes at him. "What King George will you be wantin'?" Not waiting for Edwin's reply, she picked out a long-stemmed buttercup from her tray and held it out to him. "D' you know what to do with this?"

He did and took a step backwards. She lifted her chin and positioned the flower head under it. "Do I love butter?" she asked, peeping at him.

There was no sun to reflect any yellow under her chin. The girl was an idiot. "Do you know or not?" Edwin shouted.

"No." She laid the flower back in her tray. "There's three of them in London. Or maybe more," she called back, walking away.

Three King George taverns! He should have guessed there'd be several. Edwin puffed out his cheeks; he was the idiot! And he'd no idea where he was. What now? Wander around hoping to find another King George when he couldn't be sure Smudge would even be there? Or give up and return to the cellar? Yes, that was best; he'd go back again. Streets heading south led to the Thames, he knew that. But Swallow Street branched eastwards and standing where he was he'd no sense of direction.

He'd woken up late that morning and found himself alone in the cellar. Why hadn't he listened to Joe last night, instead of pretending to know the way to the tavern? The boy did something to him; made him defensive, aggressive even. A winged insect rose from a rotting apple on the pavement. It buzzed in front of him and settled on his sleeve. He slapped it dead.

Dull start to the morning. He glanced up at the sky; overcast with no sign of sun. No help there. He'd learnt a few maritime tricks from journeys home at sea. But they involved navigation by the sun or stars. His shoulders slumped, and he kicked the rotten apple off the pavement. Smells might help. At least it was a better part of London with none of the smells of the Shambles where butchers threw out rotting meat. He straightened and breathed in, sniffing the air. As though summoned, a dray cart pulled up. Seconds later, the stomping carthorse had covered the apple with steaming dung. Edwin bolted, clutching his nose.

He halted further along the pavement. Coffee! The unmistakable smell of coffee! It was something he missed, both from school and home. With a sigh, he realised he hadn't any money. No matter, he followed his nose to the coffee house. It would be full of customers and he could ask the way to Swallow Street and wait for Smudge. Edwin pushed through the doorway.

Worst timing ever.

As soon as he stepped into the fumy, tobacco filled interior of London's most notorious coffee house he wanted to leave. But couldn't. Behind him, the door crashed back on its hinges. Uniformed, armed men of His Majesty's Royal Navy burst in intent on seizing as many drunks, lingerers and scroungers there at that moment.

'Press-gang men! Open the exit doors!'

Too late.

Edwin couldn't escape. He was manhandled back into the street; lifted by the seat of his breeches and thrown into a waiting cart.

A high-sided wagon-cart that transported felons to the gallows! Edwin shuddered as he stared at the surrounding miscreants. Not one sober one there! He elbowed himself free from the jumble of arms and legs and stood upright. The wagon lurched. Shouts and curses from the less fortunate flung to the ground. Edwin grabbed the side of the wagon and hung on.

Theirs wasn't the only wagon load that day. Two more joined them on the way to the docks where, locked in a warehouse, they waited for the tide to turn. Edwin kept his mind occupied by counting the number of press-ganged men and boys and reckoned they totalled sixty.

A good haul for the three-masted frigate out in the Thames. Could be a sister ship to the Cambridge, Edwin thought as he stood in a longboat with other captives being rowed out from shore. It was a two-decker warship, a ship-of-the-line carrying eighty pounders. On his twelfth birthday, his Uncle Robert had taken him aboard HMS Cambridge to meet Captain Hartwell, and he'd toured the ship and made a sketch of its square-rigged sails.

While Edwin studied the ship ahead, a second longboat followed behind. If he'd looked back, he would have noticed a malicious man on board guarding more unfortunates. A big sailor with a skull and crossbones ring on his finger.

Close to the frigate, Edwin glared up at the waiting crew. Treated as an honoured guest a year ago, and now, taken against his will....

"Keep in line, there!" Musket at the ready, a smooth-chinned sailor lad gave him a butt in the shoulder. Just so he knew.

Edwin stared around, eyes and ears on high alert. He had to escape. But there was no chance, roped together climbing the gangplank. And no release, until they'd marched across the mid-deck, and descended steps to the hold. Then the captain, a short sturdy man with a ginger beard, blew a whistle and summoned them to attention.

"Recruited, that's what you are," short pause. "Into His Majesty's Royal Navy. So, you can forget about loved ones, or any wenches left behind," thin smile. "Though by the looks of you—"

"Hold it there. Captain, if you please." A weather-beaten old crewman stepped forward, interrupting. "There's a storm brewing. Foresail up top don't look good to me eyes. Wants bunching."

The captain nodded, then cupped a hand to his mouth and shouted: "Top sail luffing. I need someone to climb up and fix it."

Adrenaline shot through him. "I can climb," Edwin yelled from among them. "I'll go."

"Make way for the lad!"

Edwin pushed through, gave the captain a quick nod and headed for the steps.

"Foremast sail, lad."

The captain's command followed him as he ran up to the deck and fled towards the quarterdeck companionway. Escape! Escape, Escape! Feet pat-patting along the damp wood planking. He flew past the crew. Mist giving way to rolling black clouds. Wind in his hair. Up a second flight of steps to the foremost deck.

And before him, the towering oak pole of the mast.

He positioned his feet on the rope ladder and climbed hand over foot to the first of the yards. Then up a short under-ladder to a caged platform. A scramble over the platform rails and a pause, gasping, with his feet planted.

Up the rope ladder again – to the second yard and a rest on the platform. It was worse than chimney climbing. Flues weren't exposed to the elements. The wind was freezing. It whipped hair across his face and sucked his body flat. Up again to the third yard. The ladders getting shorter, his body heavier; the wet rope stripping his fingers of skin.

"Wheheee!

Finally free! Edwin flung an arm in the air. And he gripped the mast as he swayed with the rise and fall of the ship. There were white crests on the waves and, looking up, threatening clouds as the sky darkened. Below, squinting down, he could see the upturned faces of the crew. They were only a blur.

Then he remembered the sail needed fixing. It was in all their interests to obey the captain. On a previous sailing trip, he'd watched the crew swarm along the yards fixing the canvas. He could do that; lie flat on the yardarm. Press his knees either side, grip tight, and stretch his arms….

Don't look down!

Impossible.

He cringed as a wave of fear ran up his spine. His body trembled and he couldn't move. He couldn't move! But he had to. Close your eyes, Edwin. Imagine climbing an upright pole, knees gripping, arms pulling. An inner voice, whispering. Smudge urging him on, climbing St George's Church wall… That did it; brought him back to his senses.

Compelling himself not to look down again, he crawled along the yardarm and grabbed the flapping sail. Then he inched back to the mast with the restraining rope between his teeth. Recalling a sailor's knot, he secured the rope to the mast. His eyes streamed in the salty wind and his hands chafed. But he'd completed the difficult task. His body was stiff with cold but inside – he glowed.

Meanwhile, on deck with crewmen looking on, a row was taking place.

Edwin strained to hear their words blown on the wind. Two men stood apart from the crew. He recognised the captain. The other, a big man and much taller, his face distorted, was shouting up to him.

"Come… Down… leave… be."

A sudden brightness in the sky; a spark of lightning, no more, but enough to see the twinkle of a ring.

Scurvy Sam!

Edwin clutched the mast, pressing his face to its hardness. His heart pulsed madly, and he forced himself to stop panicking. He was safe, for now. But the thought swirled in his head; he knew, *just knew,* Sam would catch up with him.

"I tell you straight, that boy be nephew to Admiral Richmorton. If happen he falls, we'll all swing for it!"

The captain clapped a hand to his sword. And who's to believe a scurvy thief like you? He's of value to me, and I have need of him."

"Aye, of more value than you can suppose!"

Edwin slipped further down the mast. The mast creaked and groaned as he stood on the first platform, but leaning over the rails he caught the word:

"… reward."

"Tell me more. It's your duty."

"I wants half. I nabbed him once before. Equal shares, Captain."

"The devil I will!" A flash of steel as the captain unsheathed his sword.

Sam let out a yell. He turned to the mast and moved fast. Before anyone could stop him, he was on the ladder, the rope rungs straining with his weight.

Edwin span round on the platform and grabbed the under ladder again. He had to climb fast. Sam was gaining on him. He reached the top rung. Sam yanked the ladder away from the mast.

His fingers still gripping, Edwin swung in air. His feet dangled free, and he kicked out into nothingness. He cried out at a sudden tug and twist of his ankle. And the world spun: – sails – Thames – sails – Thames – deck. Deck!

He was hanging upside down, ankles snagged in the ladder. Inches below him, blackened teeth and a leering face. Sam made a grab for him. His face came close. Edwin sucked in, and –

Spat straight into Scurvy Sam's eyes.

The sailor let out a bellow. His arms gave way and his grip slackened, and Edwin saw despair in his eyes as he slid down the ladder, and fell to the deck.

The crew gasped and stepped back. Sam was up. The captain shouted for someone to restrain him. But he backed to the rails and swung himself over. It was a high tide and the water deep and choppy. When he resurfaced his mouth was open and gasping. There was a rush to the portside. Sam couldn't swim.

This was his chance! Gathering strength he never knew he possessed, Edwin righted himself and untangled his feet. A cloud burst above him and rain poured down. The rain aided him as he half-climbed, more slithered, down the wet mast. Intent on trying to save Scurvy Sam, nobody saw him climb over the starboard rails.

Until –

Shouts from the crew brought notice he had disappeared. "The boy's no longer up the mast!"

"He's nowhere on the ship!"

They searched in the wind and rain while the deck slopped one way then the other.

"No sign of him."

Edwin had lowered himself down the ship's side, found the open door of a long canon, and squeezed in beside it. He stayed put, hugging himself. When he sensed there was no more activity above him, he reckoned they'd given up, thinking him drowned.

Not long after, the ship gave a shudder. Edwin covered his ears as a deafening *rattle* and *clank* reverberated through the length of the hull. The anchor chain being hoisted! The brief storm had passed, and the ship was preparing to leave.

So was he! He waited until the ship leaned to starboard, then he leapt from the canon hole into the Thames.

The water sucked him down, down, dangerously close to the hull. Kicking out, lungs bursting with effort, he reached the surface. It was an easy swim from ship to shore and Edwin struck out for Coal Harbour Wharf, an area he'd got to know with Mr Wills. Glancing back, he saw the frigate in full sail heading down river out to sea. He'd had a hand in that! And whether they'd rescued Sam or not, it no longer mattered. A demon had been put to rest.

When he reached the shoreline with its flotsam and smelly tang of seaweed, Edwin sat on an upturned barrel for a while, letting the sogginess dry from his clothes. His chafed hands and the sores on his knees didn't look too bad. He grinned to himself. Smudge would approve; 'They'll be o'right, once the sea salt's dried on 'em.'

But then, excitement over, he remembered about the reward for his capture. It was more common to advertise for runaway slaves! A small red crab scuttled past him and sank through the mud. Edwin laughed out loud. As soon as he got back to learning the trade he'd be black with chimney dust, and nobody would recognise him.

He clapped a hand to his mouth. What about Mary? A moment of qualm. Was he being selfish; not considering how worried his family may be? Edwin stared at the bustle of life around him; larger vessels out in the river, and lighter boats and barges moored side by side receiving goods to be rowed upstream. He wasn't ready to go back yet. And he couldn't allow himself to get emotional, he had to be strong. When he achieved the challenges he'd set and proved himself, he could return.

Determined, Edwin left the Wharf and headed back to Swallow Street.

Chapter 19
Bad Influences

Joe and Pete were standing outside Bess's premises. They'd seen him coming and waited as he limped up the street. His ankle hadn't been painful when he'd first reached the shore. Now, having walked quite a way, it really hurt. Edwin forced a smile to his face as he approached.

"Nothing to worry about," he said. "Cricked my ankle a bit." He shivered. It was late evening and his clothes still damp.

Pete tugged his arm, grinning up at him. "Where have you been, Ed? Did you see Smudge?"

"Let him get inside, Pete!" Joe said, opening Bess's front door. Joe gave him a sympathetic look. "It was quite a storm, you must be cold."

He shrugged.

They stood inside the hall for a moment. The house was silent. "Nobody's seen her for two days," Joe whispered, though there was no need.

Down in the cellar, Edwin went straight to his sleeping bag and snuggled inside.

Pete and Joe came and sat beside him. Pete saying he couldn't sleep until Edwin told them where he'd been. So, he sat up and related some of his story. They listened in silence, and there were no questions when he told them he'd been press-ganged. He guessed they hadn't believed him, when, too tired, he fell asleep. It didn't matter as Smudge wasn't there.

Bang! Bang!

The following morning, the sound of banging jerked Edwin awake. It came from overhead. He scrambled out of his sleeping sack and stared around the cellar. It was empty. No Joe or Pete. Edwin moved to the coal heap and glanced upwards. He put a hand to his eyes, shielding them against the sunlight. The hatch was open.

Smudge's face peered down at him. "'Bout time, too! You're coming wiv me, Ed." The hatched slammed shut.

Edwin collected his dry clothes from the coal heap and bundled them into his sack. He'd taken a lead from Smudge. 'Best keep your own goods with you; you dunno where you might end up.'

Smudge was waiting for him on the pavement

"Come on," he said, "Afore any of the mob gets back."

"Where are we going?"

"The Green Man. You'll find out what for when we gets there." Smudge said, chuckling.

Edwin wasn't too happy; the situation at Swallow Street worried him. So many unanswered questions:

"What's up with Mistress Carter?" he asked.

Smudge sniggered. "Ain't never heard her called that 'afore."

"Is she ill?"

"Dead, more like!"

"What makes you say that?"

"'Cos her housekeeper told Jake. That's why."

This was news to Edwin, so he'd been with Jake. He stopped. "Housekeeper! I never knew she had one."

"Daft old biddy. Deaf as a Dodo. She got the Quack to see Bad Bess, first thing this morning."

"Was Jake with you?" Smudge looked guarded. He rubbed his nose and sniffed.

"Jake's gone and gone in with coal heaver Wills," he said. "He's thinkin' of setting up a business with 'im."

Smudge was off again, walking fast.

The Green Man inn sign dangled precariously on the corner of an old building. Its weathered paintwork had flaked away and little remained of the walking man in his bower of greenery. The sign creaked and groaned on its single chain, threatening to crash down at any moment. Edwin stood back. But Smudge insisted they enter.

There were few customers. Three old men sat at a table, sucking clay pipes. The interior was so dim Edwin didn't notice them at first. Smudge pulled him down on a bench. A woman in a stained apron appeared. She stared at them then ducked under a low arched doorway behind the bar, and disappeared.

Smudge gave Edwin a nudge. "He'll be out in a minute."

Edwin had a sudden urge to bolt. He stood up. Then relaxed. The little man with spectacles on the end of his nose approaching them couldn't have looked more harmless. As soon as he saw Smudge, his large face split into a Chinese grin. He clasped his hands together and did a little bob. Smudge pushed Edwin forward.

"Mr Ching, this'll be the boy fer you. He'll do a good job. What d'ya say, Ed?" Smudge closed one eye in a deliberate wink.

What could he say? Mr Ching looked at him, grinning expansively, *expectantly!* Edwin opened his mouth, and a strangled *'yes,'* came out. It had obviously been pre-arranged.

Smudge slapped him on the back. "That's the way!"

What way? What was the stupid monkey on about!

Smudge tapped the side of his nose. "Art and mystery of the trade." Edwin frowned. "Along the road t' being a chummy, Ed; that's what." Edwin's frown vanished.

He followed Mr Ching through the arched doorway into a stone-floored kitchen at the back of the inn, and stopped, surprised. A large chimney stack dominated the kitchen.

"The chimney originally occupied an end wall," Mr Ching explained in faultless English, "It became a central stack when a room was added behind it, creating an annex." While Mr Ching was talking, Edwin heard drunken voices raised in argument. The sound of shouting and swearing came from the annex.

"The annex is a single storey building," Mr Ching was saying. He pointed a finger, "The fireplace is behind this one. There are two flues." So that's what it's all about, thought Edwin, relieved. He gave Mr Ching a puzzled look, however, when the Chinaman instructed him to climb up the kitchen flue and come down the adjacent flue in the annex.

"No sweeping or cleaning required. Just appear in the fireplace."

"I don't understand."

What Mr Ching said next, made everything clear.

"I have drunken gamblers in my back parlour," he said. "They are undesirable persons and I wish to be rid of them. You must creep, unobserved, into their midst, then cry out in a loud voice, 'My master, Satan, has sent me to you all!' They will panic at your black appearance and leave my premises."

Entering into the spirit of things, Edwin blackened his face and hands with soot from the hearth and prepared to climb. The kitchen fireplace was larger than the one he'd climbed in the cottage chimney. How to get up? The over-mantle was several feet above his head and the hearth was clear, with no handy logs to stand on. Nor were there any protruding bricks or rungs inside the hearth.

Mr Ching fetched a tall stool from the bar. Edwin was reluctant to part with his sack. But he couldn't risk losing it in the flue. Mr Ching assured him it would be safe with him.

No problem climbing up, just a startled encounter with a magpie as he emerged on the roof. Then a slower descent down the annex flue, and he dropped to the hearth. No one heard him. The air was thick with tobacco fumes and the poker players far too drunk. He could have sat in their midst without anyone noticing.

Keen, nevertheless, to carry out his mission, Edwin leaped in the air arms outstretched and yelled, "SATAN!" To added effect, he brandished a poker from the hearth.

They noticed all right! He was crushed to the wall in the scramble to get out. Bodies fought each other through the door to the outside yard, and he'd just recovered his breath, when Smudge appeared.

"You done well." Smudge was jubilant, "We all done well!" He yelled.

In their terror, the poker players had left the table covered in money. Smudge spread his arms and gathered up the coins, then stuffed his pockets, while Edwin filled a drawstring purse they'd left on the table. Several five-pound notes had fallen to the floor. Edwin didn't hesitate. He snatched them up and hid them inside his shirt, his heart thumping against his ribs. He'd never stolen anything before. Smudge was all for, "Hopping it quick."

Edwin's conscience bothered him; it was obviously a practised ruse. "No Smudge, we've got to give the money to Mr Ching. By rights it's his. Perhaps he'll share it, or pay us. Anyway, he's got my sack!"

On their return to the bar, a delighted Mr Ching greeted them. The Chinaman didn't ask for any money and handed Edwin his sack. He then sat them down at a table and clicked his fingers. A pot-boy appeared with two bowls of broth. Mr Ching excused himself and went to greet two men entering the inn.

The boys wasted no time in spooning up the broth. Plum pudding and custard came next.

Edwin felt a tremendous sense of well-being and beamed at Mr Ching. The little Chinaman leaned in close,

"Empty your pocketsss!" He hissed.

Edwin shot to his feet. Two men were guarding the door; the two men Mr Ching had greeted. They stared straight at him and didn't look friendly. He looked at Smudge for help. Smudge picked up a lump of bread and stuffed his mouth.

"Right decision, lad." Mr Ching snatched the £5 notes from his hand. He gasped as Mr Ching bent down and picked up his sack. Oh no! The purse! Mr Ching held the sack by the neck, weighing it in one hand. His expression said everything: 'heavier than it was!'

Smudge seemed unconcerned. Edwin was still standing. He clenched his teeth, furious with himself. He'd been outwitted! And Smudge had the nerve to sit there, his money still in his pocket, not caring what happened to him.

Mr Ching opened the drawstring purse. He looked up at Edwin. His eyes sparkled behind his glasses and he rubbed his hands together. Then the unexpected happened. Mr Ching counted out ten coins and handed them to Edwin.

Then it was just a matter of shaking hands and they were on their way. When they reached the door, however, the two men rose to their feet.

Chapter 20
Learning the Art

The two men in The Green Man Inn turned out to be chimney sweeps named Ginger and Wiley, who roamed the countryside looking for work. Edwin hadn't been too keen on joining them but Smudge had introduced them by name. Well he would, wouldn't he, being Smudge; not let on that they were going to be there! Summer months being a quiet time in the trade, Smudge said he often journeyed with the sweeps. Edwin suspected they were rascals, but he'd already embarked on the road to crime and he tried to convince himself it would be part of his learning curve.

The sweeps owned a strong horse and cart. Ginger told him he lived with a quarrelsome sister, and welcomed time away from her. And Wiley, with two former wives, four children and a one-legged father to support, was keen to travel and earn money.

"Me number two misses that was, be after the 'orse," he grumbled. "Claims 'orse be hers on account of me buying it and her at horse fair. Stupid filly weren't worth the money. Horse is though."

He and Smudge had fallen about laughing. Ginger had glared at them, and Wiley narrowed his eyes, looking serious.

Edwin spent a week or so travelling the country roads with the sweeps. They crossed the border west into Buckinghamshire where nobody knew him. He worked well with Smudge, doing his bit sweeping chimneys when needed, and loading up the cart with soot. In remote cottages and small homesteads they swept flues for the soot alone. No payment needed. The arrangement suited both sides. Ginger and Wiley had regular clients, who waited for them each summer, and the sweeps made a good profit selling their soot.

Edwin was the happiest he could remember. He enjoyed sweeping the short straight flues with Smudge, and they rarely left a job without, 'partaking,' as Smudge called it 'of good vittles.' In other words they ate well. Those were the best aspects of the trade.

After parting with the sweeps, he'd wanted to return to London.

"We gotta stay a bit longer," Smudge told him. "Cos of meeting up wiv Jake. We've got a good contract hereabouts, wot we do most summers."

Edwin groaned, 'hereabouts' he suspected, being dangerously close to Hertfordshire.

While waiting for Jake, he and Smudge stayed with a village blacksmith. The sky had been cloudy for days and the forge was a good place to rest. And in Edwin's case, reflect.

As he did now, sitting on a stool at the blacksmith's bench, writing. Smudge was out foraging for berries in the hedgerows. Edwin had told him it was his thirteenth birthday. Still unsure how long he'd been away he guessed the date was near enough; and what better time to catch up on his writing.

One sheet of paper remained. He'd filled the rest, writing chronologically, jotting things down: *lesson one: The Art and Mystery of the Trade with Mr Ching*; his first lesson in deception. The forge door was open, and a mouse stood upright in the doorway, its little pink ears directed at him.

"What about the other aspects of the trade; other so called '*mysteries!*' Shall I record them?" He was just as guilty of helping Ginger and Wiley deceive the farmers as they were and hadn't given it a single thought.

"I'm bothered now," he told the mouse. "I knew it was wrong… But I loved being involved, having friends."

The mouse twitched its whiskers and scurried away.

Edwin stared after it, chewing the end of his quill. All part of life, good and bad and he'd take the consequences.

He smoothed out his final sheet and wrote:

To understand the 'adulteration of soot,' you need to know that there are different kinds of soot. Soot from cottage chimneys tends to be of poor quality, due to the burning of wood, faggots and vegetable peelings. Cottagers can't afford coal. Consequently, rascally sweeps mix soot of poor quality with better quality soot, obtained from the burning of coal.

The mouse was back.

"Abbeys and mansion houses," Edwin said. "We get the best soot from them."

The mouse vanished.

Edwin dipped his quill in the ink and wrote several paragraphs and some dialogue. Enough. He stowed his writing materials in his sack and stood up.

The blacksmith, a jolly fellow with a leather apron flapping around his ankles entered the forge. A carthorse plodded behind him. The horse snorted and stamped its hairy feet when it caught sight of Edwin.

Edwin greeted the blacksmith, thanked him for his hospitality and left. A smart one-horse chaise stood in the yard, the reins held by a be-whiskered groom. A vision of Amos flashed before his eyes. Edwin ground his foot in the dirt. Why couldn't the past leave him alone? It seemed the longer he stayed away, the faster it caught up with him!

He watched from a distance while the groom led the horse to a water trough to drink. When the chaise departed, Edwin sat at the roadside waiting for Smudge. The warmth of the sun made him feel sleepy. And he closed his eyes and dreamed of succulent goose and chunky plum pudding with thick yellow cream....

A shadow fell across him. He looked up.

"That's your lot. Eat 'em fast, we got to be off." Smudge thrust a basket of blackberries at him.

Edwin stuffed his mouth with berries. He couldn't stop eating them. "Where are we going?" he spluttered.

"Over the hills and far away."

"What!"

"Song I 'eard once." Smudge turned to him, grinning, "I got another, what I knows all the words to. Got no time now. We'll 'ave to run if we don't get a move on!"

Edwin scrambled up, "Did you see Jake?"

"I'm meeting up wiv 'im. We've got the contract t' do Windbridge Hall and you'll 'ave t' do the kitchen chimbley."

When did he contact Jake? How did they keep in touch? Did they have a system of bongo drums! Edwin ran to catch him up. "Where are you meeting him?"

"At the Hall. We always does Windbridge, third of June."

Edwin went cold. "Is that today's date?" He'd missed his birthday, yesterday, second of June!

"Lummy, Ed, it's your birthday, that's what you said!" Smudge sounded aggrieved, no doubt thinking of the berries he'd picked.

"Of course, it is," Edwin kept his tone light, not wanting to let on. "When were you born Smudge?"

"Dunno, June or July, I fink." He changed the subject. "You bin writin' again? There was a distinct sneer in Smudge's voice. Edwin nodded. "All them squiggles and things be enough t' do yer head in!"

"Not when they mean something and you know how to do them. I could teach you." No reply. Edwin tried again, "Smudge, you're teaching me how to sweep flues. We'd be even then."

Smudge's footsteps slowed, and he started talking about his trade. In a way, it seemed to Edwin he was trying to warn him about the dangers of chimney climbing; something he'd not said much about before. And it began when he asked about Jake's crippled foot.

"He don't like no-one t' talk about it."

"No. I don't suppose he does." This wasn't getting him very far and Edwin was quite prepared to end the conversation. But Smudge continued.

"Jake were 'about your age, don't remember quite, I fink he were – when it happened." He scratched his head with both hands as though rummaging for answers. "Younger 'n me now, anyways," he said eventually.

A long silence. They had reached an imposing stone gateway, topped by a stag with antlers – the entrance to Windbridge Hall. As they passed through and starting up the short drive, Smudge finished what he was saying.

"Workhouse master 'ad jus' took me to work fer Bad Bess, when they brought him in. He were screaming, Ed. Jus' think of that! Jake screamin'! Smudge was walking backwards, facing him, eyes wide in disbelief even now after so many years.

"W, what, what happened to him, Smudge?" Edwin found himself stammering. He'd been wrong about Jake's foot.

"Fell off of the roof, didn't he? Pot give way. Foot got broke in two places, and Jake could never climb no more." Smudge halted. "But he did. He 'ad to. Nofink else for it. 'Course his foot never mended, proper. An' he weren't much good at climbing fer long." Smudge actually grinned in his face. "'S what we does fer a livin', Ed."

Smudge turned, "Could tell yer a whole lot worse," he said, as they approached the ivy-clad Hall and walked round to the back yard. "About boys wot got stuck in foggy holes, in bends in flues clogged up wiv soot. Suffocated they did. Chimbley bricks 'ad to be removed to get 'em out."

He said this with gusto, then lifted his hand and tugged the bell by the kitchen door. The door opened.

"In you go, Ed."

Chapter 21
Hazards

It seemed like miles of endless darkness as Edwin scrambled upwards in the kitchen chimney at Windbridge Hall.

'A foggy 'ole,' Smudge had called it, and he'd forced himself to enter, choking at first with the sulphurous fumes. Smudge had managed to terrify him. Funny way of helping! Perversely though, it spurred him on. He cleared his mind, concentrated and got on with it.

He'd been 'caping it', climbing corner to corner in a flue so narrow the roughness of the sides scrapped his bare shoulders. He screwed his eyes tight against the soot. The flue was the smallest he'd ever entered and blocked with soot. This is what it really feels like, he thought, sucking in his breath through closed lips. The soot poured over him, thick and soft, dislodged by his body. He didn't need his short-handled brush. He opened his hand and let the brush go. It fell below, and he could hear it bouncing off the sides of the flue with the soot, down the long straight drop to the hearth.

He stopped to rest. Cold sweat trickled down his naked body. As he'd discovered before, climbing in narrow flues was easier with no clothes. Soot collected in pockets and collars and made corners difficult to get round. As it was, soot clogged his eyebrows. How much further to the top!

'Best keep going. Keep going, Ed.' He imagined Smudge's voice whispering in the eerie darkness. Or was it the flue, sighing. Talking kept him going though he daren't open his mouth! Up, up, UP. An unbearable strain on his arms! How much longer! To his left, the feel of a bend! And, relief, relief! A travelling slope he could crawl along. Then a corner, not so easy. Brush down the soot, kick it behind, squeeze round. And up again.

Finally….

He'd reached the pot.

But it was impossible. He couldn't grip the top and haul his body through. His eyes streamed and the tears stuck to his face. He was too weak… his fingers too slippery. The pot was tall and he hung perpendicular. To relax would be fatal….

He let go.

The pain kept him awake. He thought he'd died. He couldn't breathe. Was he dead? No. He was wedged in the bend, his nose on his knees where he could smell his own blood. Edwin lifted his head and spat out a ball of soot. He had to get out but he couldn't move. Panic drove his fingers and elbows, then his arms, as he flailed about, dislodging the soot to free himself.

Jane entered the kitchen. The young scullery maid carried a bowl of water an overnight visitor had complained 'wasn't hot enough!' She crossed to the table, fuming, ready to dump the bowl down. Something caught her attention. Her hands flew to her mouth.

EEEEEK!

The crumpled heap in the hearth was barely recognisable as human.

Edwin lay submerged in a pile of soot, his right leg extending upwards. Blood trickled down his leg from his toes.

Jane's screech echoed down the lower passageways, bringing Mrs Dincome the cook, and two footmen to the kitchen. By the time they arrived, Edwin was sitting up. Jane's bowl had bounced on the floor and emptied the contents on his face. The water had revived him. But he wasn't fully conscious and the kitchen swam before his eyes in a dizzy haze. He put a hand to his face and tried to rise.

Jane backed to the wall trembling.

The cook scolded her. "'Tis only a sweep boy fallen down the flue!" Mrs Dincome turned her attention to Edwin. "Let me help you, lad. I can see your knees and your foot's bad. Any other injuries?"

He wasn't aware of *any* injuries, apart from not being able to focus. He'd been lucky. The soot had cushioned his fall, saving him from possible death. A footman helped him up, and a pain shot up his leg. He yelled. They helped him to a chair. The toes of his right foot were torn open to the bone and bleeding.

Mrs Dincome sponged him down and dressed him. She seemed surprised by his neat pile of clothes. Jane washed his face; clearing his clogged eyebrows and ears of soot. When she attempted to comb his hair, Cook slapped her hand away.

"We'll have to cut it." Edwin roused himself enough to protest. The Cook's response was sharp. "You look like a sissy with hair to your shoulders!" she told him.

Edwin shut his eyes. The kitchen was still spinning, and he no longer cared what they did to him. They fetched an upper maid, who gently washed his knees and bound his bloodied toes with clean linen. While she did so, Cook took a pair of large scissors to his hair. He sipped warm milk and tried not to notice the sooty locks littering the tiled floor. Were they his? Did they belong to him? He only came alert when there was talk of sending for medical help.

"Friends – are – coming," the words stumbled out as he desperately tied to concentrate. "Jake and Smudge – waiting, outside."

They were happy with that. Jane's face went pink at the mention of Jake. And Cook's worried frown vanished. Bess Carter's boys were regular sweeps at the hall.

Edwin put his torn foot to the ground, testing it. Then he applied his full weight. Ouch! Too painful to walk. The footman went to fetch a walking stick. When he returned Edwin thanked him and hobbled to the door.

The two women seemed reluctant to let him go. Jane relieved him of his sack, and she and Cook walked with him to the yard. As Edwin made his way down the long stone passageway with them, his thoughts were a jumble of worries. Smudge would be there. He might not be there! He was meeting Jake. Smudge said he was meeting Jake! He might not be! Smudge had left him to enter the kitchen on his own. He may have disappeared!

Outside in the yard, Edwin leaned against the kitchen wall. A deserted yard; no one around, not even a clucking hen. Everything seemed to drain away from him, leaving him limp. His head slumped to his chest.

Jane and Mrs Dincome stood in the open doorway, looking apprehensive. Then Jane brightened and pointed, "There's Foreman Jake," she shouted. "And he's got his-self a donkey!"

Edwin heard the *clop-clopping* of hooves seconds before they did. When he saw Jake and Smudge entering the yard he wanted to rush out and greet them but his legs wouldn't move. They'd come from the direction of the stable, and it looked as if Jake had purchased a young mule.

Smudge got to him first. And halted. His face puckered up with concern, "What you done to y' self, Ed?"

He opened his mouth, about to reply, when Jane stepped from the doorway and spoke for him. "He tumbled all the way down the flue." she said, beaming at Jake. "And he fell out, right in the hearth with no clothes on. And his foot's got hurt!"

Sounds like it was her accident! Edwin felt annoyed. He couldn't recall much himself. There was blank space, a blur. He remembered clinging to the inside of the pot, then nothing, until coughing up soot in the hearth....

A wave of faintness overcame him and his legs gave way. The walking stick clattered to the ground. Smudge rushed to his side.

Jake threw the reins at Jane. "Take the moke!" he shouted.

The boys lifted Edwin and half carried him to the donkey. Their good intentions came to nothing, however. The donkey, too young to be broken in, bolted. Frightened by its own success and not knowing where to run, it galloped round the yard, then stopped and kicked its legs in the air. Then set off again, finally halting and braying disconsolately.

Edwin, held up by Smudge and Jane, laughed with them as the scene unfolded.

The donkey had jerked its head at Jake as if to say; 'I'm off! You'll not catch me. Hee HEEE!'

Jake, however, had long arms and legs, and despite his crippled foot could run. It was no contest. The donkey rolled its eyes and brayed as Jake mounted him. Jake leaned forward, gripped the donkey's mane and tamed the creature by a simple act. Jake hooked his foot under the donkey's right foreleg and held it up, leaving the donkey with three legs.

Either the donkey objected to bearing Jake's weight on three legs, or their gales of laughter embarrassed him, but it worked. The donkey stood quiet while Edwin was put astride its back.

He found it more comfortable lying with his head between the donkey's ears and his foot crocked up behind him. Edwin smiled to himself as he listened to Jake arguing with the Cook. It began pleasantly enough.

"Sorry about the boy. He did a good job," she said, and she handed Jake a prearranged fee for sweeping the kitchen chimney. Jake counted the money and then asked for extra payment for the soot.

"Best soot, as you know, Misses, we take away." Jake jerked his head at Edwin. "Moke's got enough burden on his back. We'll 'ave to leave the soot. But we expects payment for it."

Mrs Dincome wasn't easily intimidated. "I'll have to ask his Lordship!"

Jake laughed. Jake's laughter was more of a creaky squeak. He turned to Smudge with a scornful look on his face. "What do you think of that, Smudge?"

"I thinks, Jake...." Smudge stopped and screwed up his eyes in concentration. "I thinks that Mistress Bess Carter'll be wantin' money fer the soot and –" Smudge jabbed a finger in Edwin's direction. "Mistress'll be wantin' re, re...." His cheeks puffed out in frustrated effort.

"Recompense!" Edwin yelled.

Jake took a step closer to Cook. "Recompense for loss of one of me boys." Mrs Dincome looked alarmed. "I've already got one of me chummies off sick!" Jake said.

Chummies? Was Jake referring to him! Edwin rallied enough to sit up.

"I'd be happy enough with some writing paper," he called out. They turned and stared at him. "On which to write. If you'll be so good," he said.

Smudge whispered something in Jake's ear. Jake nodded and followed Cook into the kitchen.

"Why's Jake got a donkey? Is he setting up on his own?" Jane asked Smudge.

Smudge took charge of the donkey's reins without replying. Edwin was also keen to find out. "Is he, Smudge?"

"Don't rightly know," he muttered.

"Yes, you do. Just tell us!"

Smudge nodded at Jane, who stood apart with folded arms looking set to wait all day. "Not s'posed to say nothin', not yet. Not till he's got all his stuff," he said, lowering his voice.

Jane overheard. "What stuff?" she demanded to know.

"A cart an'...." he broke off. Jake was coming back. He was holding a sack.

His sack!

In his semi-conscious state, he'd forgotten about it.

"The writing paper what you wanted, is in yer sack," Said Jake. "Smudge'll carry it for yer."

Back on the high road again they set off south towards London. Jake led the donkey and Smudge walked alongside.

Smudge had his sack! Edwin wondered if he should be worried. He didn't have the energy. For the moment, he just felt grateful.

Jake was in a good mood. "With payment for the soot, we'll stop over and have a bed for the night." He told them.

"Where we stayin', Jake?" Smudge asked.

"The Greyhound Inn."

Smudge danced a jig in the road.

Edwin hoped it wasn't too far. It was uncomfortable lying on the donkey's back. Shaken and bruised from the fall, the constant jolting from the donkey's hooves made things unbearable. He sat up. Now his legs dangled, and blood seeped through the open wounds on toes. He clung to the donkey's mane and bowed his head so as not to show his tears. He just had to endure the pain. But for how much longer?

Chapter 22
The Greyhound Inn

Smudge let out a *whoop*. The inn was a cheering sight. A large coaching inn, far superior to the Green Man Tavern in Camden.

The donkey lifted its head and halted.

Edwin eased himself to a sitting position. He'd either fainted or fallen asleep. Not waiting, he slid from the donkey's back. He let out a cry, both with pain and relief as he hit the ground. His foot really hurt, but it felt good to stretch and rub his back.

While Jake made enquiries about stabling, Edwin clutched his sack and Smudge's arm, and they stumbled across the inn's forecourt towards the entrance.

A stagecoach in the livery of the Royal Mail stood outside waiting departure. Its passengers, having disembarked, were taking refreshments inside the inn. They looked up when he staggered in with Smudge. A young couple got up from a settle to make way for him. Edwin smiled his thanks. The innkeeper called out to a surgeon he knew to be present, and a plump jolly looking man got up from a nearby table. The man smiled as he approached him.

"Shall I take a look?"

"Thank you, sir."

Edwin stretched out his leg, and the man unwound the bloodied linen from his foot.

"Nothing a bathing and clean wrapping won't cure," he said. A pot-boy came with a bowl of warm water. Edwin tried not to wince while he cleaned the wound.

"It'll take several days and you'll have black rings round your toes to remind you, lad," he said, giving him a grin.

Smudge handed him a tankard of mulled wine. As he sipped the warm liquid, Edwin vowed it the best he'd ever tasted. The wine made him drowsy. When Jake came to tell them he'd fixed things with the landlord, his face floated in and out of Edwin's vision. He tried to concentrate but his head kept drooping.

"Did you say just the one room?" he asked, lifting his head.

"You and Smudge, and maybe one other. You'll have t' share," Jake said, and Jake seemed to have two heads. He blinked rapidly.

"Where are you sleeping?" Edwin asked.

Smudge chipped in, "Jake don't want no room. He's gonna doss down with the moke. Ain't that right, Jake?"

"Creature'll want company," Jake muttered, moving away. "I'll get a blanket and pillow off the landlady." He wagged a finger at Edwin. "Make sure you gets some rest! Don't want you laid up more 'n necessary. Smudge and me got chimneys to do tomorra, so you're on your own." He turned and left.

Smudge sat beside Edwin and tucked into a large chunk of cheese. Edwin had no energy to eat. To keep his eyes open, he stared hard at a framed poem on the wall. He tried reading the words but only managed the last lines:

"… Her son decently clothed and restored to his mother, no longer needs creep,

Through lanes, courts, and alleys, a poor little sweep."

Edwin's eyes closed, and he fell asleep.

When he woke the following morning, Edwin didn't remember being put to bed. He must've slept well. The truckle bed next to his was empty. Smudge must be out working. There was another occupant in the room, however. A man lay on his back, emitting little puffs of air through his lips. His bedding had slipped to the floor exposing his nightshirt.

Edwin sat up with a jolt. A nightshirt! When did he last wear one? He shrugged and tested his toes on the floorboards. They only hurt a bit. Perhaps he could climb tomorrow or at least help. And he managed to stand at a bowl in a back room, splash water on his face and refresh himself.

He took his writing materials with him and ventured down to the front parlour. The Inn being closed to non-residents until noon he sat on his own at a bench table and started writing.

"Oh look, dearest; it's that poor, poorly boy!"

Edwin lowered his eyes and began a new paragraph. A young couple were approaching.

"May we join you?" the young woman asked.

He chose not to hear, but there was no escape.

"We saw you here last night." They sat opposite him, their faces smiling, keen to please.

"Yes. You were very kind." Edwin remembered they'd given up their seat on the high-backed settle.

"Is your foot better?" The young man inquired, his forehead wrinkling in concern.

"My toes are recovering well. Thank you." He sounded defensive, not really wanting to talk.

The innkeeper came and placed a bowl of fruit and some bread on the table. He exchanged a few words with the young husband and wife and then turned to him.

"I see you're handy with your letters. How's your mathematicals?"

"Fair enough, sir."

"Only my accounts need a going over, and my misses and me aren't too good at figures. So, if you've a mind to help us."

Edwin smiled, "Gladly."

The innkeeper rubbed his hands and pressed his lips together, looking pleased. "There'll be full board and a bed, for two nights," he said.

When he'd gone, the young man pushed the bowl of fruit towards him. Edwin put his pen down. They each took a piece of fruit and munched companionably for a while.

"May I ask what you're writing?" The young woman asked.

Edwin changed the subject and replied instead, "That poem interests me." He pointed at the framed poem on the wall.

"Well of course, it would. It's a sad story."

"Do you know anything of the circumstances? Was it a true story?"

"Oh yes, the story's well known around here. The mother's name was Marjorie Davis and she lived in London. She was the wife of a soldier—"

"A foot guard, rank of private…" interrupted her husband.

"She had a baby and six-year-old son. While her husband was away, she asked a neighbour to look after the children when she went out charring and washing clothes. One day, on returning home she was horrified to find that her neighbour had gone and taken the boy with her. When she discovered the woman came from Leeds, she set out from London, carrying her infant." She stopped and drew in her breath in a sigh.

Her husband continued, "She walked all the way and eventually arrived here, at this inn."

"Yes, she did. And she went into the kitchen," said the young woman smiling at Edwin, "to ask about lodging. And there, sitting at supper, she saw a chimney sweep and his boy. The boy rushed to her, crying, *That's my mother!*"

Edwin, caught up in the story, wanted to know more.

"The master sweep said he'd bought him from a ragged woman, he'd found beating a child she claimed was her son. She said she'd a long way to go and couldn't cope with him. And she offered to sell the boy to him as an apprentice. There's a happy end," the young woman added. "Some Christian-hearted individuals raised a subscription for Marjorie Davis and her son."

The young couple smiled at each other and stood up. Edwin thanked them. They shook hands, wished him well and left.

Edwin stared down at his writing. He'd been recording his tumble down the flue. It could wait. The story he'd just heard made him think about little Pete; six years old and frail, spending his childhood in a coal cellar. He and Joe, where were their parents? … he wondered. Why hadn't he asked them about their lives? Too caught up in himself that's why! His toes niggled with pain.

Edwin filled his quill with ink, took a clean sheet of paper and wrote: *The Marjorie Davis Story,* and he drew a line under the title. It took time to write. He'd just added the poem when—

Three silver coins appeared. Slapped down on the table by a soot black hand.

Edwin looked up. Smudge.

Smudge just stood there not saying anything.

"What's that for?" It seemed an obvious question to ask.

"For me name."

Three silver pennies for his name? It was a fortune! What did Smudge mean? Then it dawned on him. "You want to write your name?"

"Course." Smudge gave a nonchalant shrug.

He didn't want Smudge to pay him. Of course, he didn't. But he did understand the climbing boy's pride. Edwin handed back two of the coins.

Smudge scowled, "I give you three."

"I'll only take one. As repayment, Smudge, for the penny you left me."

Smudge grinned. "Best go an' wash me 'ands then."

Chapter 23
Misunderstanding

Edwin sat up in his makeshift bed. His corner in Bess Carter's cellar showed signs of being lived in and it made him feel more at home. He'd copied the climbing boys' habit of curling up inside an empty sack and used his own sack as a pillow.

He and Smudge had arrived in darkness the previous night. Jake had gone off to stable the donkey in Major Foubert's yard and not returned. No light showed in Bess's upstairs room and Edwin had risked entering with Smudge through the front door. His toes were still raw, and he didn't fancy a slide down the coal heap.

To his great relief he saw that Pete was fast asleep. The frail little boy had been on his mind a lot since leaving the Greyhound Inn. So much so, he'd decided to keep a close eye on him. Joe may be a protective older brother, but he still felt uneasy about him. Before settling for the night, he and Smudge had found out that Bess was better. And Joe warned them that their mistress had rallied enough to notice Smudge's absence.

For now, though, Smudge was already up and on his way out. Edwin called after him, "Wait, I'm coming with you."

"No point, Ed. You'd be no good."

"Why not? I'm fit as you!"

"Not talking 'bout your toes. It's treacle chimneys I'm doin' and they're slippy and dangerous. I've got t' get in mistress's good books. It's payday tomorrow. She won't give me no money else."

"So, let me help you." Edwin picked up his sack.

"I ain't taking you, Ed! So don't ask me." Smudge scowled and turned to unlatch the door.

"Where are Joe and Pete?" He'd noticed they weren't there.

"They've had t' go to Windsor."

He grabbed Smudge's arm. "Windsor Castle?"

"That's the one." Edwin's grip tightened. Smudge prised his fingers free. "Nofink t' do with me, Ed. They asked fer Pete special. We done chimbleys there afore. They ain't so bad. Bit of a trek there, lessen mistress took 'im."

"Did she? Did she take—"

"Dunno."

Edwin sank down on his bed, his eyes fixed on the closed cellar door. He was alone.

Abandoned. There was light enough to see, and he stared round the empty cellar. Loneliness before was nothing to feelings that overwhelmed him now. The rumble overhead of carts and carriages about their business; the crying out of wares from costermongers, and the chatter and laughter of milkmaids passing, added to his misery. Everyone doing something, going somewhere. Wanted. The climbing boys had accepted him as far as it went. But he could have been a stray dog, tolerated as a novelty. It hadn't mattered him being there. Edwin pulled his knees up and clutched his head... Then he straightened and shook himself. What had come over him! What gross conceit to think he'd change anyone! And how pathetic, wallowing in self-pity....

He got up. So, what now? Take his sack and leave? No, he'd promised himself he'd look out for Pete.

The cellar door opened and Joe appeared. Joe's face and hands were grimy with soot. "Hello, Ed."

The boy's expression gave nothing away. Was Joe surprised or pleased to see him? Edwin struggled to decide.

"Are you all right?" Joe asked, "If you're hungry there's food in the kitchen. No-one's in."

"Where's Pete?" He sounded confrontational, almost accusing, but was powerless to stop himself.

Joe looked uncomfortable. "Look, I don't know what you've got against me but what my brother does, is my concern not yours!"

They glared at each other.

Fair enough, Edwin thought. Joe was right, the problem was him. He couldn't think sensibly. He pondered the reason. Put it down to anxiety, whatever. They stood face-to-face

"I still want to know!" Edwin spoke first.

"Why?"

"I'm making it my business."

"Oh, really!"

For a moment, he got caught up in the brightness of Joe's blue/grey eyes. Then the blood rushed to his face. He grabbed Joe by the shoulder. The boy flinched.

"You know as well as I do," he said, his teeth clenched in anger, "That Pete is too young and too frail to climb flues!" He tightened his fingers, then let go. Joe sucked in his breath. Was Joe going to spit in his face! No. The boy stepped back and turned away. Joe was trembling! Edwin paled, drained of emotion.

Keeping his distance, Joe turned towards him. "I wish you'd understand," he said. He spoke quietly with a certain tension in his voice as though trying to make him see sense.

"Pete wanted to go, and mistress took him. She was shorthanded with Smudge away. Mr Rose, the master sweep with the contract for Windsor Castle has no sons, but he does have three daughters. They've always swept chimney flues for him, and they're good at the job. Better than some of the boys I know," Joe added, making Edwin think, so that's it: he's keen on one of them! Then Joe said something that made him fume.

"One girl is sick with fever and mistress is helping out," Joe said, turning to go.

"*Mistress* is helping out!" he shouted, as Joe lifted the latch. "It's little Pete doing all the work!" Edwin yelled after him.

Outside, Joe moved fast. But so did Edwin, dead set on keeping him in sight. He'd put his mind to something and nothing was stopping him! They traversed several streets and cut-through alleyways. Joe resorted to a jogging run, but couldn't shake him off. The distance between them shortened. Joe was tiring.

Then he disappeared. Edwin halted. A large warehouse blocked his view, but he guessed where Joe was. Edwin swerved to avoid an oncoming chaise and tore across the road. Rounding the warehouse, he saw what he remembered so well – The Fleet, with its towpath and riverside reeds.

Joe was there, by the river.

Edwin hurled himself forward, bringing Joe to the ground. The boy let out a strangled gasp, then wriggled and squirmed under his weight. It was like pining a slippery eel. He tried it once, fishing with Mary, both of them struggling with the net. He sensed Joe was no fighter. Neither was he. If he exerted himself, he could overpower the boy. What then? They rolled, clutching each other to the river edge. And Joe struggled free.

Edwin lay with his face in the mud. He heard splashing from the river and lifted his head. So much for determination and resolve; Joe had slipped away and was swimming strongly. He examined his feelings. Was he crazy! Or foolish? Yes, that's exactly how he felt, foolish!

Edwin's sudden recall of Mary may have conveyed itself to her. For the moment Edwin came to his senses and rose from the mud, Mary was on her way to the same riverside spot. She hadn't been near the river for two weeks. Confinement indoors had been her punishment for bad behaviour at the family gathering. When she finally pleaded that Rats needed exercise, her father relented.

Since seeing Edwin with the strange boys and buying his shoes at the Chandlers, her cousin's whereabouts remained a mystery. On the public front, there was no further news. Lord Robert, incensed by his adopted son's disappearance, had taken on matters himself. He had placed additional adverts. All offered a 'substantial' reward to anyone with information about Edwin Richmorton, thirteen-year-old 'runaway heir' to a fortune.

On his arrival back in England, and greeted with the distressing news, her Uncle Robert had stormed through the new mansion, demanding to speak to his wife. And Elizabeth had taken the blame. 'Why the Devil hadn't she taken more care of him?' he'd demanded to know. He'd listened with growing impatience to her excuse she'd been 'endlessly preoccupied with getting her new mansion ready for his approval.' And tears had no effect.

Mary got all this from her mother; her Aunt Elizabeth having come around to tell Charlotte and shed more tears. Tears, according to her mother, not for Edwin, but frustration because Robert had not commented on their magnificent new London home.

Mary was delighted to see her uncle. He'd not only dismissed her aunt's young blackamoor, and paid for the boy's apprenticeship to a shoemaker, but Lord Robert needed her help in finding Edwin. She was good at portraiture and he wanted Edwin's likeness. Mary did her best, but the last time she'd seen her cousin, his dark curls were tangled beyond his shoulders, and his face filthy with soot. She couldn't portray him like that to the public. Consequently, she delighted and upset the family by sketching him the way he used to look. She even added the scar above his eyebrow.

She needn't have bothered, it didn't matter whether her sketch of Edwin was accurate. The response was huge. Lure of a large reward from an Admiral of the Fleet attracted half the poor of London. The sheer number of leads and so called 'sightings' kept two footmen staggering to and fro all day carrying letters and opening doors to callers. Her aunt and uncle even heard Edwin was spotted on a rooftop in Buckinghamshire! Elizabeth had gasped in disbelief.

"Preposterous!" spluttered Lord Robert.

Mary's father also brought news of a scurrilous man, answering to the name of Sam, who'd entered the bank and intimidated staff by demanding a reward saying he knew of Edwin's whereabouts. Lord Robert dismissed the claim. The man was a known thief and drunkard, paid by unscrupulous sea captains to press-gang miscreants.

It was up to her now, Mary decided. Excited to be out again, she trotted Rats up the towpath. She was looking for the chimney sweep fisherman her mother's maid had told her about. Someone was swimming in the river; a youth with short hair. A vague memory came into her mind she couldn't quite capture; had she seen him before?

She pulled on the reins. Rats stood quiet while she watched the boy turn and swim to the water's edge.

Mary smiled. She lifted her hand and waved. She recognised the slim figure of the boy sweep she'd met in Islington. Joe, the older of two brothers who'd helped when she'd tumbled from Rats.

She dismounted. As the boy came towards her smiling, she noticed he was fully clothed. His feet were bare beyond his clinging cropped trousers. Remembering his trade, the thought flashed through her mind that a bathe in the river would clean both himself and his clothes. Water poured off his narrow shoulders, and Joe's clothes clung to his body.

Mary *gasped!* A sudden coldness came over her.

Joe was a girl!

The smile left Jo's face. She hugged her chest and turned away.

Mary pulled a light rug from her saddlebag. "Here take this," she said wrapping the rug around Jo's shoulders. "It might smell of Rats," she joked, hoping to relieve any awkwardness. It did.

Jo turned and gave her a lopsided grin. "You won't tell anyone, will you?"

"No. But it'll soon be obvious!" Jo looked rueful.
"Does it matter? You being a girl, I mean?"

"Masters prefer boys, if they can get them. They don't like boys and girls mixing. Girls get blamed for being distracting and creating bad habits." Jo grinned as she rubbed her hair dry. "Me and Pete are on our own, and this way I can take care of him."

"Have you no parents?"

Jo shook her head. "My father got press-ganged into the navy. We heard later that he'd died at sea. He was a tenant farmer." She smiled and her voice softened. "I loved climbing the orchard trees, that's why I don't mind what I do now." She sobered again and patted Rats's neck. "We lost the tenancy cottage. Then mother had a fever. She died a year ago."

How calm and resigned she was, and so brave, Mary thought as she led her pony up the towpath with Jo walking ahead.

"My cousin Edwin is an orphan," she called out. "He's run away and we're worried about him." Jo turned. She said nothing for a moment, then asked:

"Is he about my height, with dark hair? A bit above himself?"

Mary sucked in her breath, hardly daring to hope. "Yes," she said.

"Number three Swallow Street, Bess Carter's address. We live in the cellar. Mistress doesn't know he's there. Nor does Ed know I'm a girl." She gave a quirky little smile. "We don't get on," she said.

Mary closed her eyes and hugged her pony's neck, light-headed with relief. Three Swallow Street, Carter, Swallow Street, she repeated to herself. Out loud she enquired further about Edwin:

"How did he get to be with you?"

"Can't answer that one." Jo frowned as thought trying to remember. "I think he met Smudge and Jake in Hertfordshire. Then he turned up one night on his own," Jo told her.

This began to make sense to Mary. "Does your mistress have a contract to sweep chimneys in St Albans?" Mary recalled finding Edwin's medallion in the cottage fireplace.

"Quite a few, yes. Pete and me don't go north of London."

"What are you called?"

"Jo."

"Josephine?"

"And our surname is Waters."

Mary glanced at the river and laughed, "Not a difficult name to forget!"

They'd reached the end of the towpath. "Do you have a good memory, Jo?" Jo nodded.

"You're Mary Wilde. You told us."

Mary smiled. "If you're ever in need of employment, come to us at Clare House, Islington." She shook Jo's hand. "Goodbye, Jo. I can't thank you enough."

And they parted.

Chapter 24
Rescue

On leaving the river, Edwin aimed to hurry back to Swallow Street, thinking Pete might have returned. But thick mud clung to his feet making them heavy, and the toes of his right foot throbbed. He'd forgotten about them when racing after Joe. They needed a good wash. And Edwin trudged up Ludgate Hill remembering the standing water-pump at Cheapside.

When he arrived, nobody waited. He thrust his head under the pump, grabbed the pump handle and cranked it down hard. A few seconds pause and the water gushed out dowsing his head and shoulders. He gasped and pulled back shaking his head like a dog. That's how he saw himself; little more than a beast. If only he could wash away the shame of his fight with Joe!

He'd concentrated on cleaning his toes. They weren't too bad. The healed skin remained unbroken, and he liked the black marks circling his toes; he'd regard them as battle scars! Edwin combed his hair with his fingers. It felt good being clean and back in control. The area was familiar, and not too far to Swallow Street.

As he passed the entrance to Milk Street Edwin heard raised voices. He walked on and then stopped. A prickly sensation at the base of his neck, a premonition made him turn back. It sounded as though someone was in danger. At the end of the street a crowd had gathered in front of the Taverner's Arms.

They stood gawping and pointing. "There's a young boy in the flue, and the chimney be breaking up."

Others took up the cry, "He'll be crushed to death if someone don't get him out."

"Whose boy is he?"

"Carter's boy. He be one of her boys. The little 'un."

Edwin heard them, and he rushed forward elbowing his way to the front of the crowd. Rough hands tried to force him back. But he prized himself free and darted into the tavern. And halted.

The fireplace had collapsed. The hearth no longer there! His stomach knotted in fear as he scrambled over rubble lying in the doorway, a single thought tormenting him. Why? Why Pete? For he knew, he knew for certain that the boy in the flue must be Pete.

Swirling soot and brick dust clogged the interior of the tavern making it difficult to see. Edwin coughed and spluttered. Tears squeezed from his eyes and rolled down his face as he forced himself to study the chimney. An end wall chimney, with two fireplaces; one above the other. Two flues! The ground floor fireplace had collapsed to the floor. No hearth. No way in.

He glanced upwards. A stone slab poked through the rafters. It was the hearth in the room above! Edwin spun round. In less than a minute he was up the stairs and across the bedchamber to the fireplace. The brick structure had crashed down. But a space under the projecting stone lintel! Enough to squeeeeeze under...

"Pete! Where are you, Pete? I'm here. I'm coming." His voice went nowhere in the choking gloom. But he smelt something. He breathed in. A smell he recalled. Gun powder! There was danger here. He yelled Pete's name again. Nothing, no answering call. He was in the wrong flue. A thousand curses! There was a hole and a hint of daylight above him. Only a short climb.

Edwin reached the top and the edges of the hole crumbled away as he climbed out on to the roof. He remained on his hands and knees and gazed around. The chimney pots had fragmented and what remained of the roof littered with terracotta and broken tiles. And the gunpowder smell was stronger. There must have been some kind of explosion, he reasoned. And still no sign of Pete. His stomach ached with worry and he wanted to howl! What could he do? The only thing left to do.

Edwin lowered his body into the adjacent flue. The chimney *groaned* with every movement. A sound of *splitting*, and cracks appeared in the masonry. He daren't move. His heart pounded loud enough for anyone to hear and—

"Ed, Ed, you came for me." A cold little hand grabbed his left foot.

A whisper, but Pete's voice. Tears welled up behind his eyelids. Edwin gasped with relief, Thank you God!

He hunched his shoulders and peered down. Below him, he just made out the top of the little boy's head, matted with soot and chimney rubble.

"Of course I did. Are you hurt?"

"… noise and… and… I can't climb."

"Pete, hold on as best you can. I'm getting you out."

The grip on his foot tightened, and he braced himself as little Pete hung on and he dragged him inch by inch up the flue. He didn't know how he managed it. But somehow the chimney held, and he seemed empowered with extra strength.

They were on the roof now. Edwin clutched Pete to him, to stop him from falling. The little boy was deathly pale with closed eyes. Mid-day sun blazed down on the tiles. He shifted to shield Pete's face from its glare and the little boy's lips parted. Pete was breathing! For a heart stopping moment Edwin had wondered if he was still alive.

The crowd spotted them from below and burst into cheers. Edwin, concerned about Pete, jerked his thumb high in the air. He hoped they'd recognised the victory sign, and give the exhausted child time to recover.

No such luck. Rescuers were on their way. They placed a long ladder against the end wall of the tavern, and a man climbed up.

Alerted by the sudden movement, Edwin looked towards the parapet. A square face with bulldog-like features appeared. The face split into a toothy grin. "Well done, lad. I'll soon have 'im off your hands."

"Stay where you are!" Edwin's voice rang across the rooftop with such authority, the man stayed put. A moment passed. "Leave us. I'll bring him down when he's rested."

The face disappeared.

Pete hadn't moved. The little boy lay heavy across his lap and Edwin judged him asleep. The best thing for him, he thought. And he glanced again at the parapet and protruding ladder and smiled. He'd won a small victory.

A *honking* sound made him look up. Geese, in vee-shaped formation, flew low across the sky towards them.

Pete's eyes flicked open, "Are the geese going home?" He whispered. Edwin smiled down at him and nodded.

As the flock continued their journey, they reminded Edwin of his own home and the time he'd been away. With merging days and nights only the church bells marked their passing. And his thirteenth birthday had come and gone.

Pete was gazing up at him. "Ed, what's your real name?"

"Edwin Richmorton." He was happy to tell him.

Pete looked content, but still hadn't moved. His lips parted again. "Do donkeys go to heaven?" Edwin nodded, yes. "Will you tell me a story?"

Edwin pondered a moment then he gazed out across the jumble of rooftops to the horizon. "Once upon a time," he began. "In a faraway land, there dwelt an English man called James. He lived with his wife Helena in a big house called an Embassy. They had one son, a privileged child who didn't go to school. Tutors came to the Embassy and taught him to be a gentleman." He paused. Pete's eyelids were drooping. "When he was old enough, the boy's mother took him to England for their holidays. Sometimes they stayed with his father's older brother, and sometimes they stayed with his father's sister, an invalid. His father's brother was a Lord and served as an Admiral of the Feet, and he married a charmed young lady called Elizabeth."

Pete was asleep.

Just as well, Edwin thought, his life was no fairy tale. Everyone adored his Aunt Elizabeth, but she was so unlike his quiet intellectual mother she overwhelmed him. He found her difficult to love, preferring Aunt Charlotte and his Cousin Mary. A painful thought struck him and he screwed up his eyes. What did Mary think of him now? What could she possibly think, seeing him like that with Smudge? And he'd been so rude. He'd barely spoken, not explained... he had to make it up to her.

163

He opened his eyes. The sun seemed less intense, and he reminded himself that he wasn't the weak boy she'd known before.

They brought up a blanket and carried little Pete down. Edwin watched him go. He waved goodbye, and they took him to St Thomas's Hospital. He was too dirty to accompany Pete and they turned him away.

Edwin sat on a bench in the street while a tavern girl wrapped his toes in a soiled rag. She was non-too gentle but kindly and he stopped trembling.

A row took place around him. They blamed the landlord. "Too mean to call in the sweep," they shouted.

"I've done it before," he told them, "And no harm."

Edwin leapt to his feet. "No HARM!" he yelled. They let him get close to the landlord, to glare at him eyeball-to-eyeball.

"I only fired a shotgun up the flue to loosen the soot," he said, backing away.

Edwin drew in his breath. He calmed slightly, but his eyes glinted and he deepened his voice. "I still demand to know about Pete!"

"The boy was there in the street," said the landlord. "He told me he'd come back from sweeping and his mistress had given him money for a pie. Did he want another? I asked him. I needed someone to climb the flue, make sure of the chimney, didn't I?"

The landlord reached in his pocket for a purse of coins. He held out the purse. "For you and the lad, and for saying nothing."

Edwin dashed the purse down, scattering coins. The onlookers cheered and slapped him on the back. As he walked away the landlord was scrabbling for coins in the gutter.

If he focused on collecting his sack, he could go somewhere quiet and write, Edwin decided. It had helped before with worrying thoughts about the trade. His mind in a daze, he continued on to Swallow Street.

"Whoo! Stop there, Ed!"

A donkey and smart handcart pulled up alongside him. Edwin recognised the young donkey. It caught his attention, trying to nibble his toes. He jumped away. When he looked up, his mouth fell open. Jake! It was Jake, dressed as a gent! Not the cut of a Daniel Porter, but fitted out in breeches, waistcoat and tailored coat, his long slim legs encased in knee high boots, Jake looked the part. Furthermore, he was grinning. He'd never seen Jake so happy.

"What d'ya think, eh!" Jake threw his arm wide, inviting him to examine his latest purchase. A handcart maybe, but a good size and light enough for the donkey to pull. His jaw dropped even further when he saw the lettering painted on either side of the cart. It read:

'WILLS & SON Small-Coal Merchants, late of 3 Swallow Street.'

Jake chuckled. "Bess give her blessing," he said. "Not that she'll 'ave much more to say in the matter. Reckon she's had it. She give Pete money for doing the Windsor flues, then she went an' collapsed in the hallway. They're with her now, the vultures; waiting for her to gasp her last and steal what they can." He got down and stroked the donkey's ears.

Edwin stared at the lettering again. Wills & Son, it made little sense. He turned to Jake and raised his eyebrows.

"Happens, coal heaver Wills be my father. Found out a few weeks back. Wills has always looked out for me, and we gets on. Never knowned me mother. Bess Carter took me in when I were a young 'un." He paused and scratched his chin. "I 'ad wondered if it were her."

This was astonishing news, but there was more. Jake, who spoke few words, now had much to say! Edwin couldn't get a word in, and he so wanted to tell Jake about Pete. Jake's next revelation, however, left him speechless.

"That posh young Miss turned up at Bess's. She helped with the lettering on my cart, so I'd get the spelling right."

A sudden chill came over him. "You, you mean… Mary?"

Jake nodded. "Said she was your cousin, and I give her your sack."

"What!" He stepped back, and in doing so collided with a little girl bowling a hoop. The child ran crying to her mother.

"I done you a favour, Ed. Like I said, the vultures are in the premises, and they'll soon have the cellar done over and take what's there." He removed a scrap of paper from his pocket.

"She give me this, to give you." Jake grinned, "Not much of a likeness!"

It was a torn 'wanted' advert. Edwin frowned. It contained an etched likeness of him! He studied it closer.

Scribbled across the top were the words: MEET ME AT THE COAL WHARF. Mary.

"When did she give you this?" Edwin asked.

Jake removed a timepiece from his waistcoat pocket. *Jake* with a timepiece! Things were getting crazier by the minute. "I reckon, she left about an hour ago," Jake said, pocketing his watch.

He then mounted his cart, flicked the reins and was off down the street.

Still feeling stunned Edwin watched him go. Then he remembered he'd not told him about Pete. Poor little Pete, he wished he could have gone with him. Edwin wiped his eyes with his sleeve. "They'll look after him, there's nothing more I can do," he muttered to himself. And he fingered Mary's note and remembered his sack. Mary had it. No point in going to Swallow Street.

Edwin turned about and headed south to the Thames and Coal Wharf. He ignored the shooting pain in his toes and ran rather than walked. His sack contained his writing. He had to get it back!

Before setting off for Coal Wharf, Mary had stabled her pony at Major Floubert's. She was welcome at the riding school where Rats now enjoyed the company of other ponies. He even let novice riders lead him around the yard. Rats liked being appreciated.

Mary sat alone on the wharf steps. The dampness of the stone seeped through her riding skirt, and she felt uneasy with no chaperone. She'd been waiting some time for Edwin, not knowing if he'd come or if he'd received her message. She stood up. For something to do, she brushed mud from the hem of her skirt.

Edwin noticed her first and approached smiling. It took some effort, but he wanted to show he was pleased to see her, and that things had changed since they'd last met. She looked surprised then shocked, her eyes darting from his shorn hair to the dirty rag round his toes. And he told her about climbing the cottage chimney, and the friends he'd made and things he'd seen and done. She said nothing, just gazed at him with a puzzled look, which didn't help. He dried up, his voice cracking.

"But why, Edwin? She said at last. "You've not explained why."

He turned away, muttering, "It was something I had to do." Then louder, almost shouting; "I had to prove myself, Mary!" He understood her frustration but couldn't explain further. She'd have to wait and read his memoirs.

Edwin leaned out over the wall. To stop himself falling, he gripped the rough stone, his fingernails still grimy with soot. Several feet below, the wharf steps were awash with coal sludge from the barges. The Thames was rising. A change in the weather brought a stiff breeze. Sea gulls circled and swooped, calling out, squabbling for titbits among the debris. His mind slipped back, remembering the mud larks working the riverbank.

Edwin shivered. He spun round. "Mary, where's my sack?"

"I've left it at Major Floubert's. It's safe with Rats, in his stable." Edwin held her eyes in a worried look. "Please come home," she said.

Edwin pulled himself upright. "I will, I will come back," he told her. "But I need my sack."

Mary smiled. Her first smile since they'd met. "I've found your medallion," she said. "It was in the cottage fireplace; the one you told me about."

A lump came to Edwin throat. He swallowed hard.

"Where is it?"

"At home. I could get—"

"No," he interrupted her. "Please keep it until I return. Thank you, Mary." No more to be said. He was grateful it hadn't been lost forever. He'd always love and value his medallion but he didn't need to have it with him. He could manage without it.

"Let's move," Edwin said. "You'll catch your death by this poxy river."

Mary laughed and kept close as they ran across the cobbles. Edwin guessed she was thinking his aunt wouldn't approve of such language!

Before they reached the riding school, Mary stopped to smooth her hair and re-arrange her skirt. At that moment, a passing stagecoach slowed down to round the corner. Edwin couldn't help himself. He darted forward and bared his teeth, grinning idiotically at the passengers.

Mary kicked his shin with her boot, "Edwin! Remember who you are!"

"I know, I know! And that's why I did it." He gripped her arms, willing her to understand. "It wasn't enough, being a toff... All right," he shouted, seeing her frown. "I mean a young gent!" He let her go.

Mary grabbed his head with both hands and kissed his forehead. She pulled a face. They both laughed. He must have tasted of sulphur.

At the stables, Edwin patted Rats on the neck, then he grabbed his sack, saying, "I'm not going back with you now. I've things to do. I'll come on my own, later."

"How much later?"

Edwin didn't say. As he left the yard, he turned and gave Mary a wave. "Don't worry, Cousin," he shouted, "I'll be back, and you have the word of a gentleman." He felt emotional leaving her; but there were still things to do.

Chapter 25
Prodigal Heir

The air was balmy in old St Pancras Church yard, and a robin perched close to Edwin. Seeking somewhere quiet, he now stood beside a tombstone, writing. He'd chosen a table-like family tomb wide enough to spread his papers and place his ink. Had he known the deceased family's name he would have asked permission, posthumously:

My esteemed Sir and Madam, I have no desire to disturb you, only that I may sit awhile and write my memoirs.

Edwin grinned at the fantasy – their names having long faded into obscurity.

He'd begun by writing about his fall down the flue and subsequent injuries, and then in more detail about his stay in the Greyhound Inn.

"I've written about facts, and some of my feelings," he informed the robin." The robin flew to the ground and cocked its head. Edwin tucked his throbbing toes out of sight.

In fading light on his last sheet of paper he wrote about the landlord and his wife and the way they'd looked after him. He'd enjoyed helping them with their accounts and they'd treated him with respect. He appreciated their respect; it cheered him knowing his learning helped other people. Something worth remembering, he reminded himself.

Edwin rolled up his papers and secured them with twine. He hadn't finished; he couldn't write about Pete. It was too upsetting, and his eyes swam with tears. Mary had helped him decide. He'd experienced life – more than he ever imagined, and it was time to go home. He stood for a moment, heaviness in his chest as he remembered Smudge.

The robin flew up and joined him on the tombstone.

"You'd be anyone's chummy, cocky little thing like you! If you see Smudge, tell him from me, I tried," he said. He'd done his best to become a chummy. He felt sad, but not bitter, in fact, it occurred to him he could help the trade when older.

"Do something about narrow flues, redesign chimneys – insert small openings with doors in impossible bends!" He gleefully told the robin, getting carried away.

The robin opened its beak, chirped twice and disappeared.

Edwin shouldered his sack and with spirits high, left the cemetery without looking back. When he'd entered the cemetery earlier, the gravestones reminded him of his parents' deaths and the fact they had no tomb on the estate. Their names were placed on an obelisk instead. Then the memory had faded, and he'd thought about other events; happy memories of time spent together.

Edwin braced himself to be resolute, but walking the city pavements jarred his feet and he lost the rag from his toes. A stout stick would've helped, he thought as he hobbled across Bedford Square. He felt light-headed through want of food and couldn't remember his last meal. And he was heading for Richmorton House; his aunt's new mansion, where he'd have to explain his absence and shoulder the consequences. Edwin comforted himself with the thought that at least for now, he knew what to do with his life.

When he reached the mansion, the wrought iron gates stood wide open. A large coach emerged from the drive. It was led by two black horses driven by a liveried groom.

Edwin gasped. Emblazoned on the side of the coach was the Royal Coat of Arms and in gilded lettering, the name, Daniel Porter. Inside the coach sat the master sweep architect himself, head lowered consulting a drawing.

Had his aunt invited Daniel to the mansion to build a fireplace? Edwin wondered.

'In the dining room, made of the finest Carrere marble,' Elizabeth had informed Lord Robert. *Adding that, 'Daniel had promised to return, at a convenient date to check the flue.'*

Nor did Edwin know that the gate was left open for him. Mary having arrived some time before, sending the family, the staff, everyone into panic with her news. Edwin had been found. He was returning! *'Prepare! Prepare!'* Elizabeth had shot into action. A special feast must be prepared for the prodigal son and heir.

Inside the gates, a shape loomed to one side of the lawn. Edwin stiffened. In the twilight, the outline was unmistakable. It was a pagoda, like the one his parents owned in Turkey. He remembered their last meal together in the summer pagoda before boarding the *Nancy May*. Edwin backed against the railings. He turned and pushed his face into the cold iron. It helped. Negative thoughts dragged you down. He was stronger now.

A positive thought came. Was the pagoda built in memory of his parents? He'd once sent his relatives a childish sketch and his Aunt Elizabeth had thought it a good likeness. Edwin pulled away from the gate. Had it been installed for him! The notion made him tingle all over.

A footman waited at the pillared front entrance. New to the job, he stepped forward as Edwin approached.

The door flew open.

Mary rushed out. She grabbed his arm and dragged him inside. They were all there, in the hall, waiting. Mary's parents were there, Charlotte supporting his aunt Elizabeth, who fluttered her handkerchief and almost fainted. It was the shock of seeing him! The line-up of new servants gave a collective gasp before discretely melting away. This was fortunate. It spared him the horror of being introduced.

Edwin shuddered. It was too much to bear. He stared down at the blue-green swirls in the marble flooring, wishing they would spiral him away to watery depths.

Lord Robert took command. "Welcome home, my boy." His uncle slapped him hard on the shoulder, no doubt pleased to think he'd been out in the world, 'earning his stripes.'

Elizabeth came to her senses. She rushed forward to hug him, then staggered back. "Oh, my poor dear boy!" she cried, catching sight of his feet. Both feet were swollen. His damaged foot had turned purple, and blood oozed between his toes.

He stuttered a few reassurances, but it was useless, his words drowning in instructions.

"Robert," said his aunt, "Send for a physician and a barber-surgeon, and someone to attend to him. He'll need a thorough washing, and some clothes and rest. He must have rest. We must get him upstairs. No, perhaps the library – we could set up a bed. Oh, no, too inconvenient! His room is ready, oh dear, what shall we do, it's in the East wing!"

Edwin sank to the floor his head spinning. Waves of sickness overcame him and he couldn't focus. He started gagging. Mary came to his rescue.

"Aunt Elizabeth, get a gardener to carry him upstairs!" She knelt beside him and pillowed his head in her lap.

Edwin didn't remember being carried upstairs, and he drifted in and out of consciousness for several days. A physician attended and diagnosed severe blood poisoning from his foot. He was also malnourished and covered in sores. Rest was called for and he was not to be disturbed. Consequently, his Aunt Elizabeth's grand celebration feast was postponed.

When he ventured downstairs, Edwin asked to be left alone in the library. "To finish writing," he explained.

His uncle and aunt were patiently waiting. He knew they were anxious to know why he'd run away and where he'd been, and they needed to know. He'd have to tell them soon. What to say? How to explain?

He waited for a quiet time with no one about, then opened a conservatory door at the back of the mansion. To forestall any worries about his absence, he gave a message to one of gardeners for his aunt, and left the grounds.

He'd decided to visit Mary.

In his role again as Edwin Richmorton, he hailed a passing carriage and enjoyed the ride. A three-mile walk to Clare House, Islington wasn't an option. Although his foot was better, his new shoes pinched, and he was in a hurry to see his cousin.

Mary gave him a hug, declaring he looked more like his old self again.

"I'm not staying," he said. "I've come to give you this." He handed her his rolled up memoirs. "Don't show them to anyone. Not yet. I want you to read them first."

Mary looked puzzled. "Where did they come from?"

"They're mine."

"What are they?"

"Didn't you look in my sack?"

Mary shook her head. "No."

Unbelievable, Edwin thought; he would've done! "They're an account of my time with the climbing boys. I wrote it down," He told her.

"Really! How wonderful!" Edwin grinned sheepishly; Mary looked so thrilled.

"I can't wait! I'd love to read them. Why me first? Shouldn't your Uncle…?"

"Some of it's in Latin," he interrupted. "And I know you'll understand. You saw me with Smudge and Jake. And you helped Jake." Mary blushed. "My uncle and aunt will never believe me, if I just tell them," Edwin continued. "After you've read it you could help me explain. Please, Mary."

She gave him a steady look, then said: "I'll read your papers, but you must promise me something, Edwin. I'll only help if you let Aunt Elizabeth give you a welcome home feast." She ignored his glare. "Everyone was terribly worried, and Aunt Elizabeth does love you. You saw the pagoda. That was made for you, hoping you'd feel at home. You owe it to her, Edwin."

He shrugged, Oh well. He gave her a smile and turned to go.

"No, sorry. Don't go yet," Mary called out. "I've, I've got to tell you something, and I don't want to upset you—"

"I'll do it." A voice interrupted her; a voice he'd heard before! Edwin spun round. Joe had entered the room. Upright

173

and slim with cropped fair hair. But a different Joe – wearing a *dress*. Jo carried a sewing basket under one arm.

"Hello, Ed." She took a step closer and held out her hand.

It remained suspended. His jaw locked, and he couldn't move. The riveting blue/grey eyes were those of Joe. But...

Jo smiled, "I had to pretend to be a boy. It was the only job where I..." Her voice faltered, "I could look after Pete." Her eyes filled with tears.

Something greater than shock grabbed his heart. He took her hand in his, "Tell me, Jo," he whispered.

"It's Pete. Pete died."

"NO. No, I saved him!" He clutched her shoulders and shook her. "I saved him, Jo!" The basket dropped to the floor.

"When they got him to the hospital, he was already dead," she said.

He released her.

Edwin stood with his head bowed. The tears welled up and soaked his face and kept coming. Jo wiped them away with her apron. He felt no shame. It was right for him to cry – for himself and for Jo. He'd known all along and so had Jo. Pete wasn't destined to live long in his world. He glanced up. Jo stood there, stoic, brave.

"Pete asked me if donkeys went to heaven," he said.

"What did you tell him?"

"I said they did."

Home again, Edwin sat in the pagoda and went over things in his head. He'd managed to smile when Mary explained about her first meeting with Jo and Pete, and Pete falling asleep on her pony. And he was happy for Jo. It cheered him knowing Mary's mother had offered her a job as personal maid.

'My hands are rough,' Jo had said 'But they'll soften. My mother would be pleased; she taught me how to sew.'

Edwin found his aunt in her marble hall. She was placing a cupid in one of the alcoves. He smiled at her and said: "I love the pagoda. Thank you. You're very good to me."

Her face went pink, and she asked if he was hungry.

"I could eat a feast!" he declared, rubbing his stomach.

"My dear Edwin, I couldn't be more delighted! Now you must accompany me to the library. Your uncle and I have something we wish to say."

Lord Robert sat in his Admiral's chair next to his favourite bust of Jupiter. He remained seated, but he fixed Edwin with a benevolent look saying:

"I have begun negotiations with Dr Forsythe." His uncle paused, cleared his throat and continued. "Dr Forsythe of Westminster School. You could attend as a day scholar. What do you say to that?" His lips expanded in a smile.

Edwin had already decided on a future career. "Would I be able to study architecture, sir?" he said.

"Well damn me! That's a fine notion, Elizabeth. What d' you make of that?"

Elizabeth said she thought it very fine, indeed. Then she looked aghast at her husband, "I'll need two days, at least," she said.

"What's that, my dear?"

"Edwin's home-coming feast. I must prepare."

And she did. Untried servants were not to be trusted and old retainers, particularly cooks, dispatched in carriages from the Hertfordshire manor. The new kitchens, indeed the whole house was active.

Edwin retired to the pagoda.

The great day arrived. What his aunt couldn't control, what she didn't foresee was the weather. The summer so far had been hot. Following Edwin's summons to the library, the weather changed. A grey dampness descended, and on the day of his feast it became cold and rained.

His aunt was agitated. "I can't have my guests getting cold. A fire must be lit."

Finally. All was ready. The new dining room looked its best with a table of shining perfection, groaning with food. Chandeliers flickered with candlelight. A maid knelt in the fireplace.

"Is it lit?"

"No M' lady. I can't get no spark t' come."

"Hurry, fetch a gardener."

He arrived with a bundle of faggots. Elizabeth clapped her hands as flames leapt up the flue. The gardener left the room. The moment he'd gone, the flames died.

And smoke descended.

Elizabeth ran to the window. The carriages were arriving. Smoke was drifting across the room! The feast would be ruined! She put her hands to her mouth and screamed.

Servants rushed in. What could they do?

Edwin heard the commotion. He was in his bedroom, arms crossed over his chest contemplating his new waistcoat. Then he smelt something. Smoke! He practically flew downstairs. Servants crowded outside the dining room door. They parted to let him through.

A quick glance was enough. Edwin seized a jug of water from the table and poured the contents over his head. He doused a napkin and tied it around his mouth and nose. The long-handled shovel might be useful. He tucked it in his waistband.

Edwin jumped into the hearth and trampled the embers, thankful for his boots. He then had to climb. What he'd find in the flue didn't enter his thoughts. He'd never extinguished a chimney fire, but Smudge's voice was there, in the gasping smoke, whispering what to do. No flames further up. He stopped. His fingers met a blockage above his head. He turned the shovel and pummelled the rubble with the handle. Loose masonry fell to the hearth.

Unexpectedly, his aunt helped save the feast. Recovering from the shock of seeing his boots vanish up the flue she'd instructed servants to hold a cloth in front of the fireplace. Consequently, Edwin struggled out from the cloth to general astonishment and much applause.

Not for one moment had he been afraid. He was pleased to be treated as a hero, of course. But what happened after the feast mattered most. The fire was lit, the feast went ahead and his aunt overjoyed by the admiration she received. Speeches were made, and everyone merry with drink when—

A footman appeared.

Elizabeth rose from the table. There was a whispered exchange, Lord Robert was consulted, and Edwin summoned to the hall.

His aunt gave him the news.

"Edwin dear, there's a boy outside. Somewhat ragged. He wanted you to have this." She handed him a scrap of paper.

SMUDGE. His signature, written in capitals. Edwin's eyes misted over.

"Do you wish to see him, dear?"

"What did he say?"

"Nothing much. He asked to see his Chummy."

Edwin's heart leapt with joy and he did something he'd never done before. He hugged his aunt and kissed her.

The End

Glossary

Jollyboat	:	Small boat suspended from the ship's stern for use in an emergency.
Rhino	:	Cockney slang for money
Primers	:	Latin grammar books
Vampire Gowns	:	School uniform, black gowns
Portmanteau	:	Suitcase with two compartments
Brine	:	Salt
Chaise	:	Light two-wheeled horse drawn carriage with folding hood, for one or two people
Hawkers	:	Street Traders who call out the name of their goods for sale. 'Chestnuts all at a penny a score (twenty).'
Penny	:	Silver penny, worth two copper halfpennies or four farthings
Curds & Whey	:	Lumps and liquid in cheese making
Coal Riggers	:	Sailing ships transporting coal
Lighter Boats	:	Large heavy flat-bottomed boat
Piking	:	Flues claimed to be unclimbable were swept upwards as far as possible and the remainder left.
Pits And Scars	:	The smallpox disease left patients with pits and scars in their skin from healed pus

		filled blisters
Scotching	:	Descending a flue in turn using knees and elbows
Papists	:	People following the Catholic faith. Supporters of the Pope.
Pounders	:	Artillery – long gun mounted on warships
Luffing	:	Loose flapping sail
Chandler	:	Equipment supplier for ships and boats. Also sold tallow or wax candles and soap. And equipment for other trades
Sheen	:	Used to split straw when straw plaiting
Tankard	:	Drinking mug made of pewter or silver with hinged flat lid
Grand Tour	:	Travel around Europe and the Mediterranean by the wealthy to 'improve' themselves, learning about art and culture abroad
Artefacts	:	Various items, ornaments etc.
Faggots	:	Bundles of chopped wood for kindling- lighting fires
Dropsy	:	Drowning by a build-up of fluid in the lungs
Quack	:	Con-man medic, posing as
Settle	:	doctor, or selling medicine without any training. Long wooden seat with high back and sides.
Charring	:	Working for payment, cleaning other people's houses.